BUG SCOUTS

CAMP OUT!

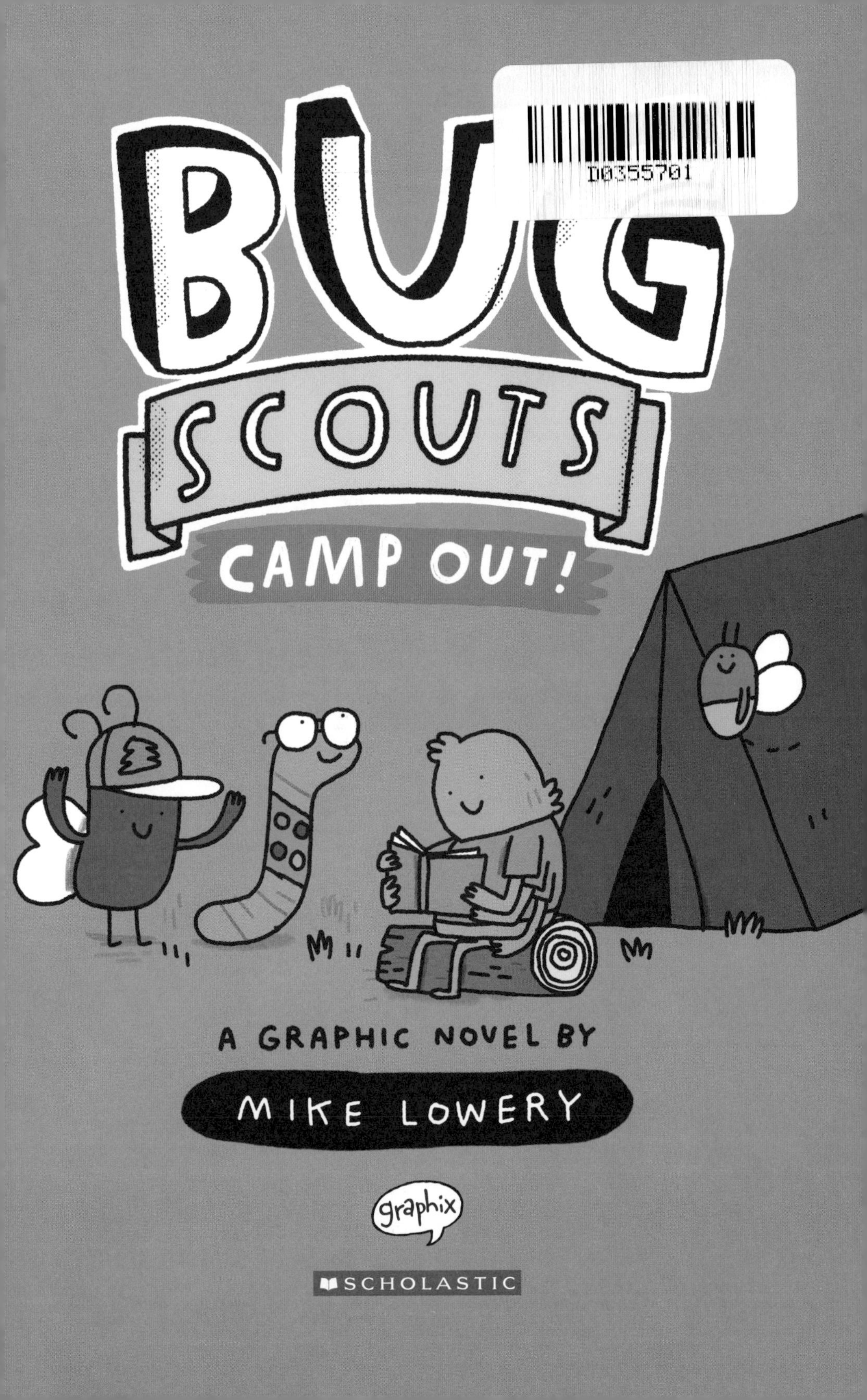

A GRAPHIC NOVEL BY

MIKE LOWERY

graphix

SCHOLASTIC

For Caleb

All rights reserved. Published by Graphix, an imprint of Scholastic Inc., *Publishers since 1920.* SCHOLASTIC, GRAPHIX, and associated logos are trademarks and/or registered trademarks of Scholastic Inc.

The publisher does not have any control over and does not assume any responsibility for author or third-party websites or their content.

Library of Congress Cataloging-in-Publication Data Available

ISBN 978-1-338-72635-0 (hardcover)
ISBN 978-1-338-72634-3 (paperback)

10 9 8 7 6 5 4 3 2 1   22 23 24 25 26

Printed in China   62
First edition, October 2022

Edited by Liza Baker and Rachel Matson
Book design by Doan Buu
Creative Director: Phil Falco
Publisher: David Saylor

CONTENTS

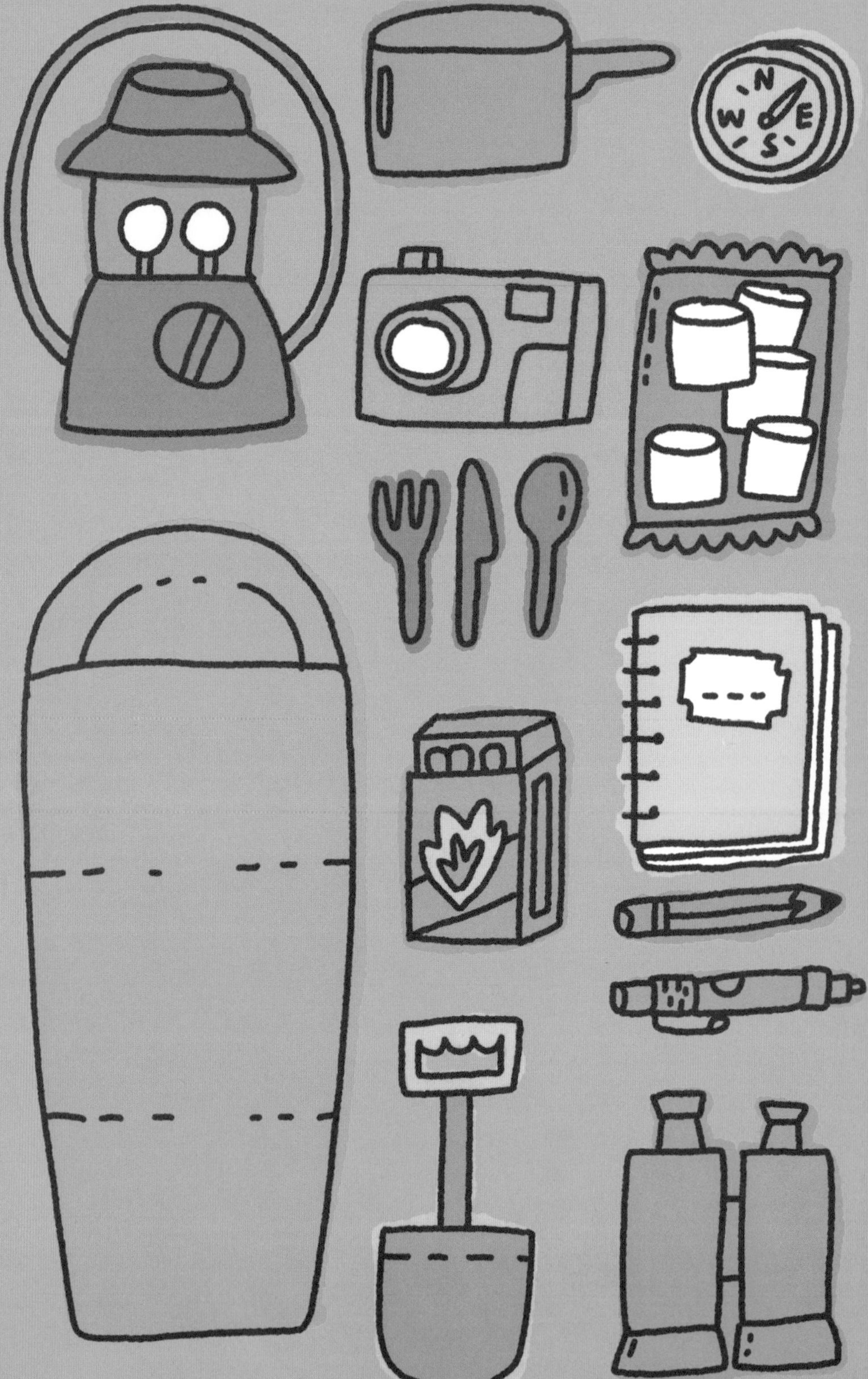
N
W
E
S

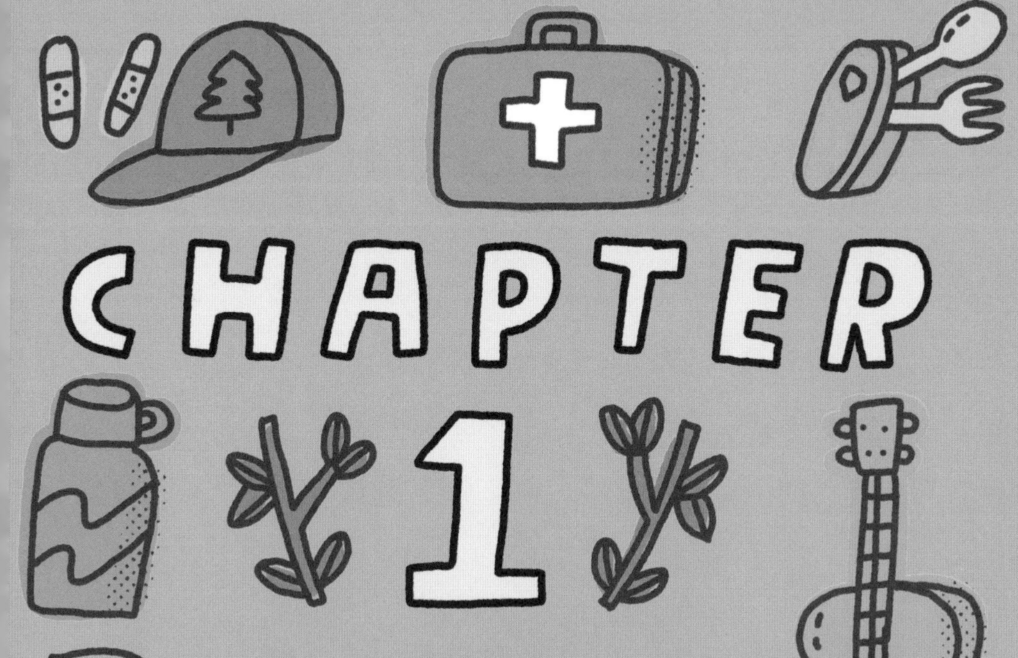

CHAPTER 1

GETTING PACKED

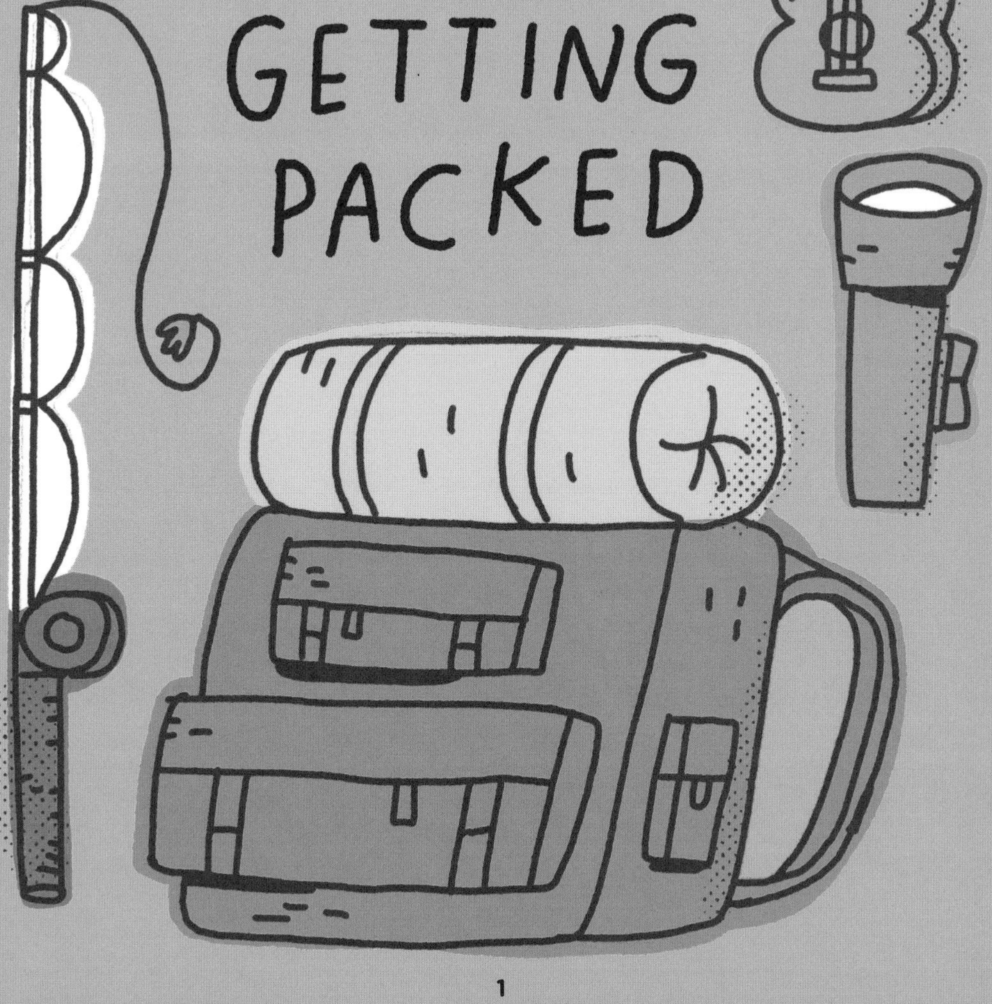

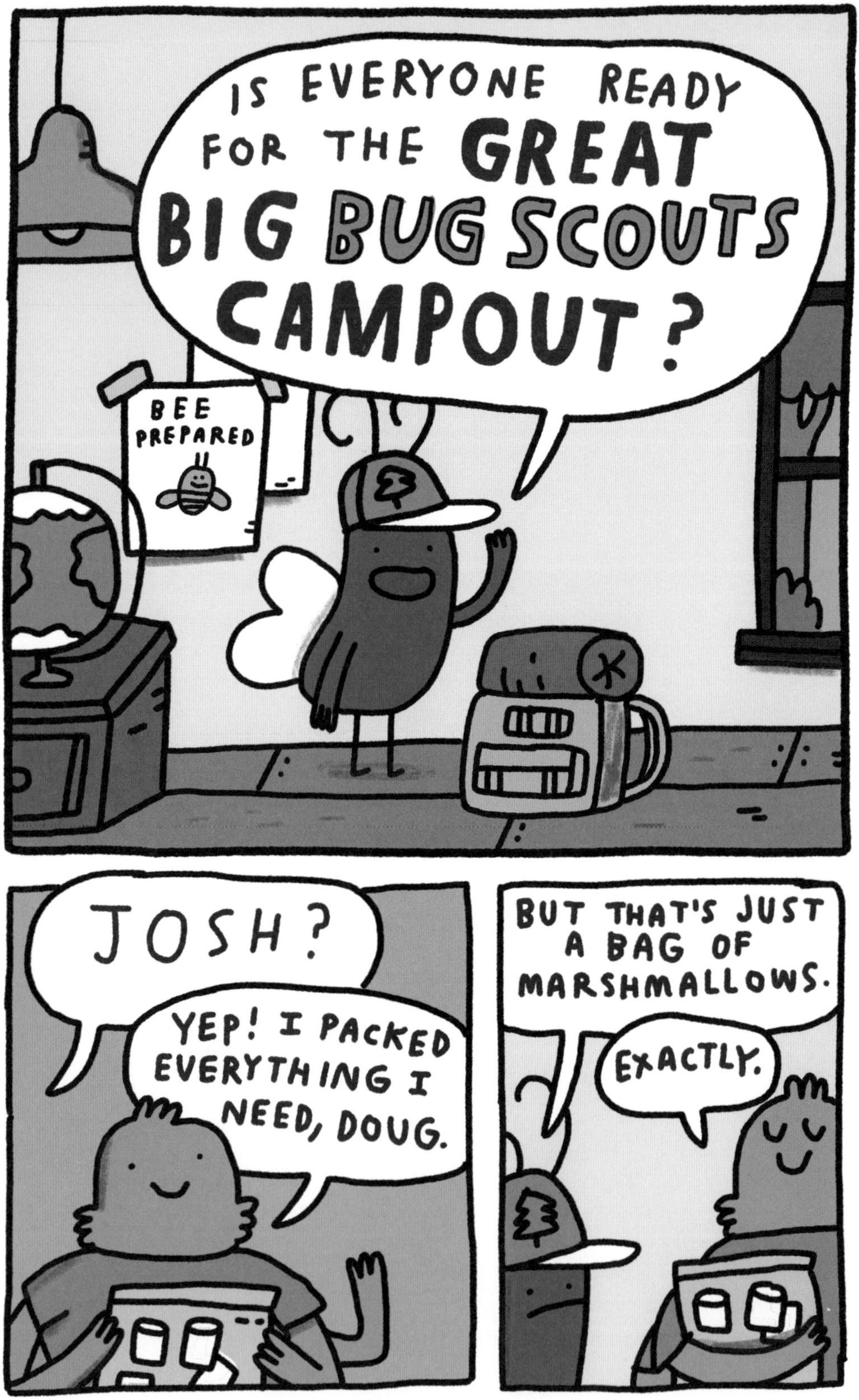
IS EVERYONE READY FOR THE GREAT BIG BUG SCOUTS CAMPOUT?
BEE PREPARED
JOSH?
YEP! I PACKED EVERYTHING I NEED, DOUG.
BUT THAT'S JUST A BAG OF MARSHMALLOWS.
EXACTLY.

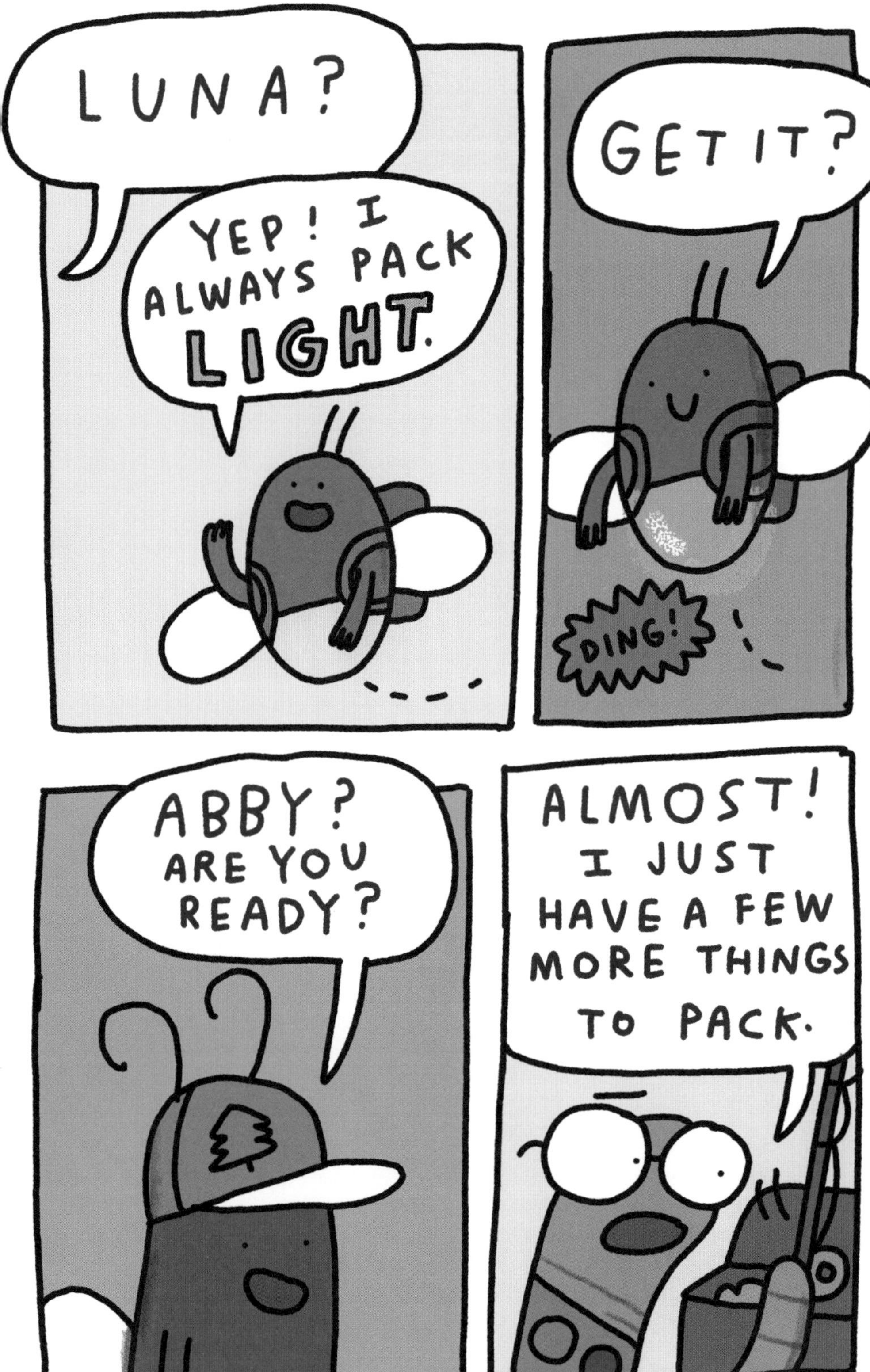
LUNA?
YEP! I ALWAYS PACK LIGHT.
GET IT?
DING!
ABBY? ARE YOU READY?
ALMOST! I JUST HAVE A FEW MORE THINGS TO PACK.

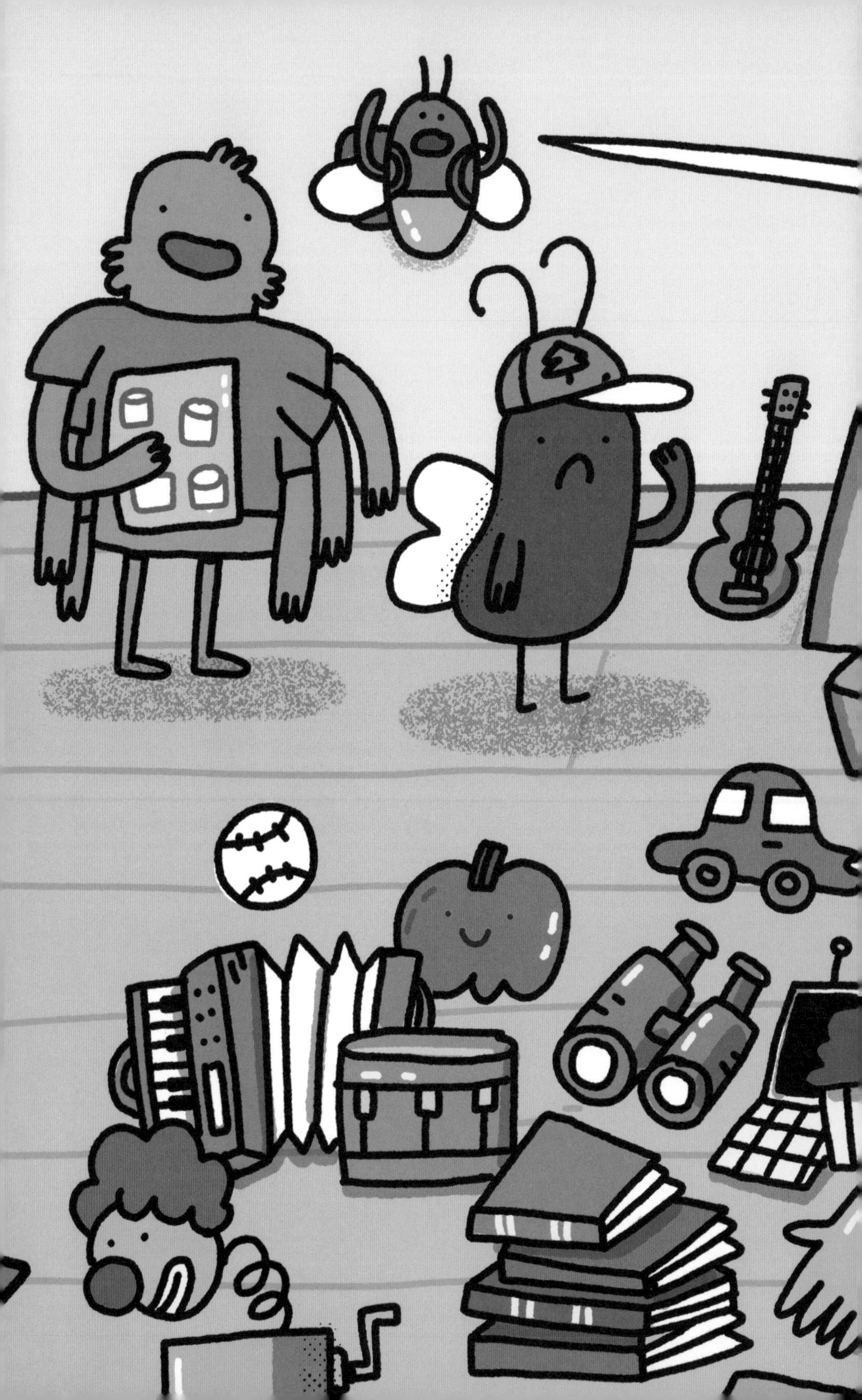

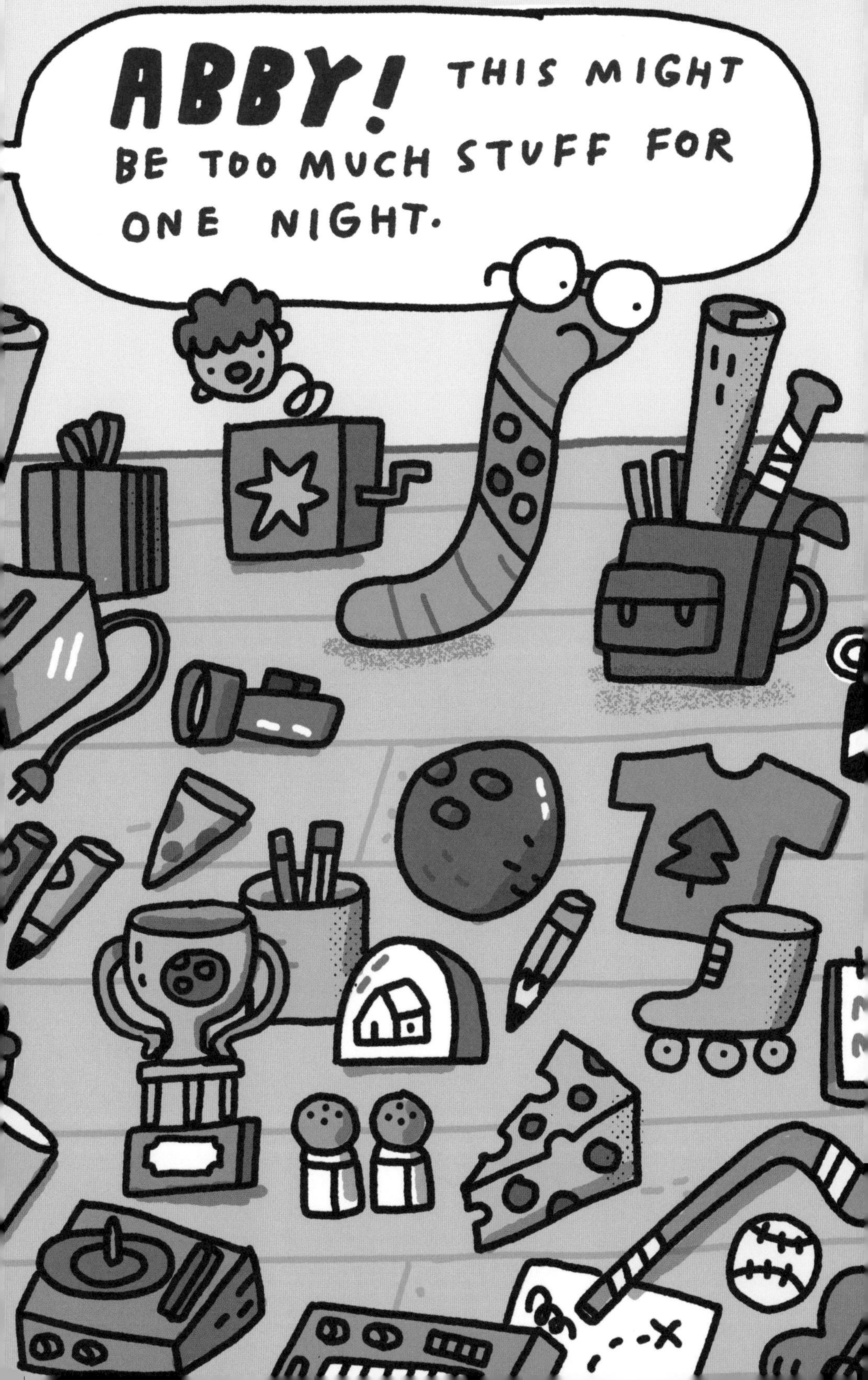
ABBY! THIS MIGHT BE TOO MUCH STUFF FOR ONE NIGHT.

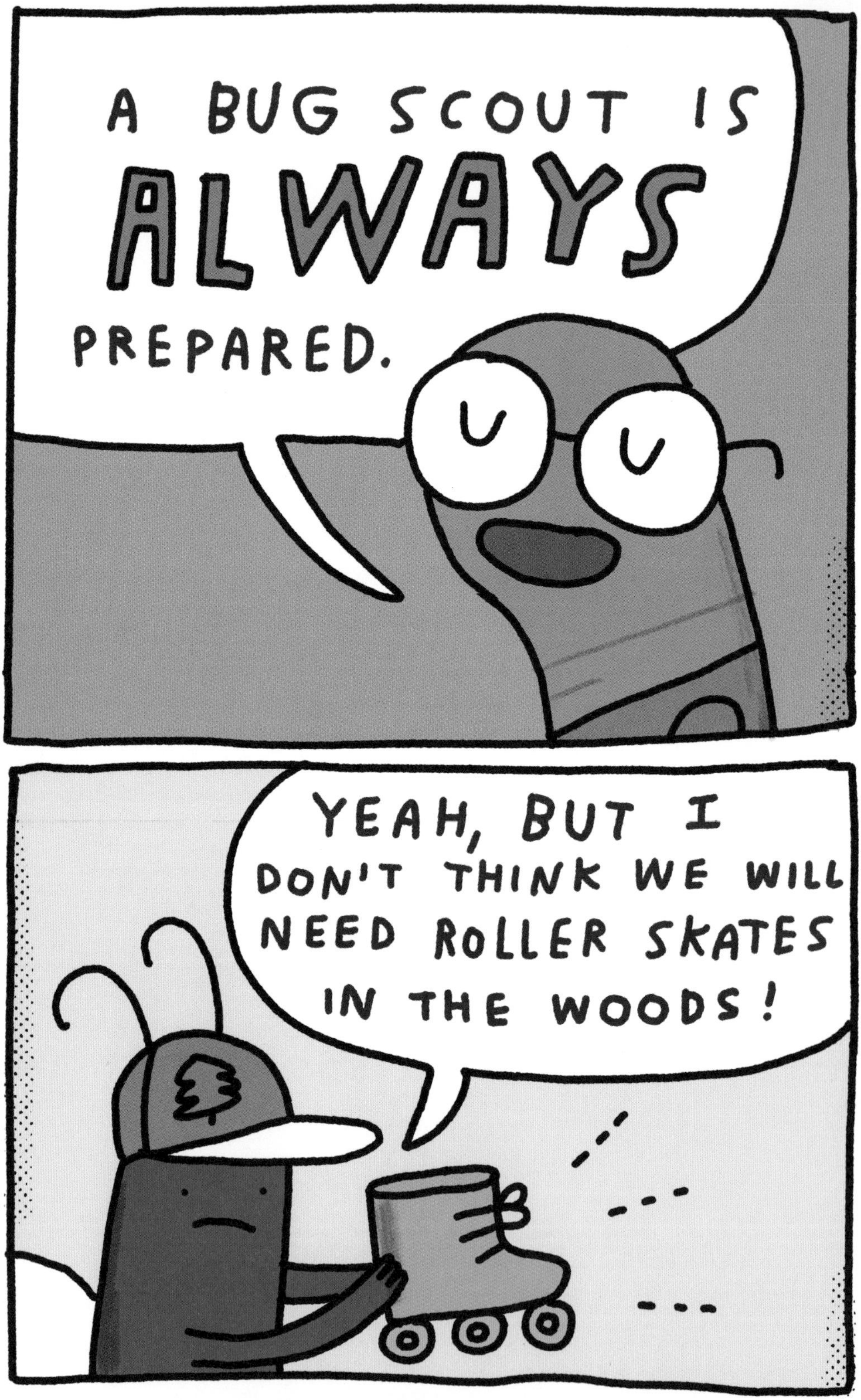
A BUG SCOUT IS ALWAYS PREPARED.
YEAH, BUT I DON'T THINK WE WILL NEED ROLLER SKATES IN THE WOODS!

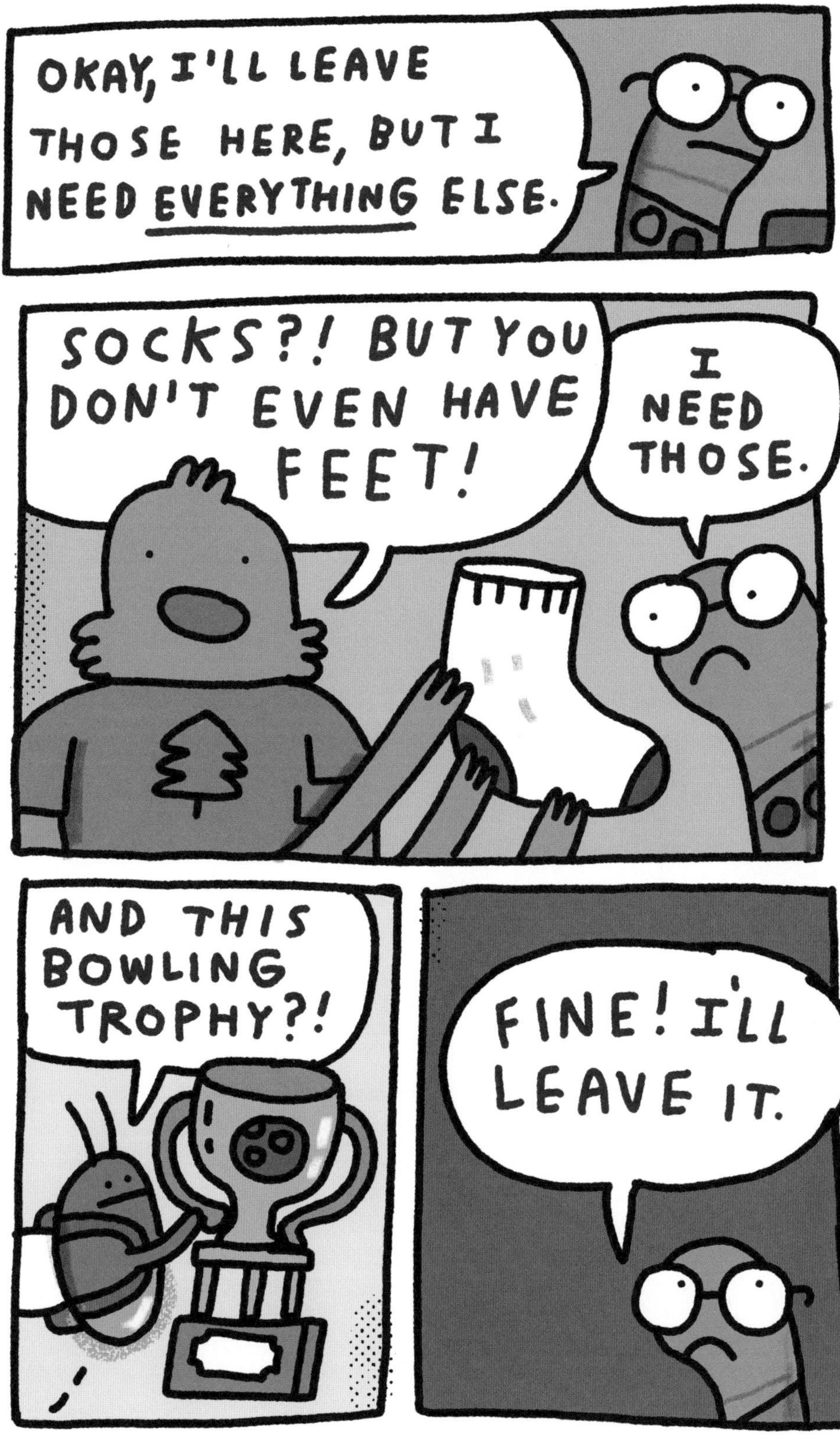
OKAY, I'LL LEAVE THOSE HERE, BUT I NEED EVERYTHING ELSE.
SOCKS?! BUT YOU DON'T EVEN HAVE FEET!
I NEED THOSE.
AND THIS BOWLING TROPHY?!
FINE! I'LL LEAVE IT.

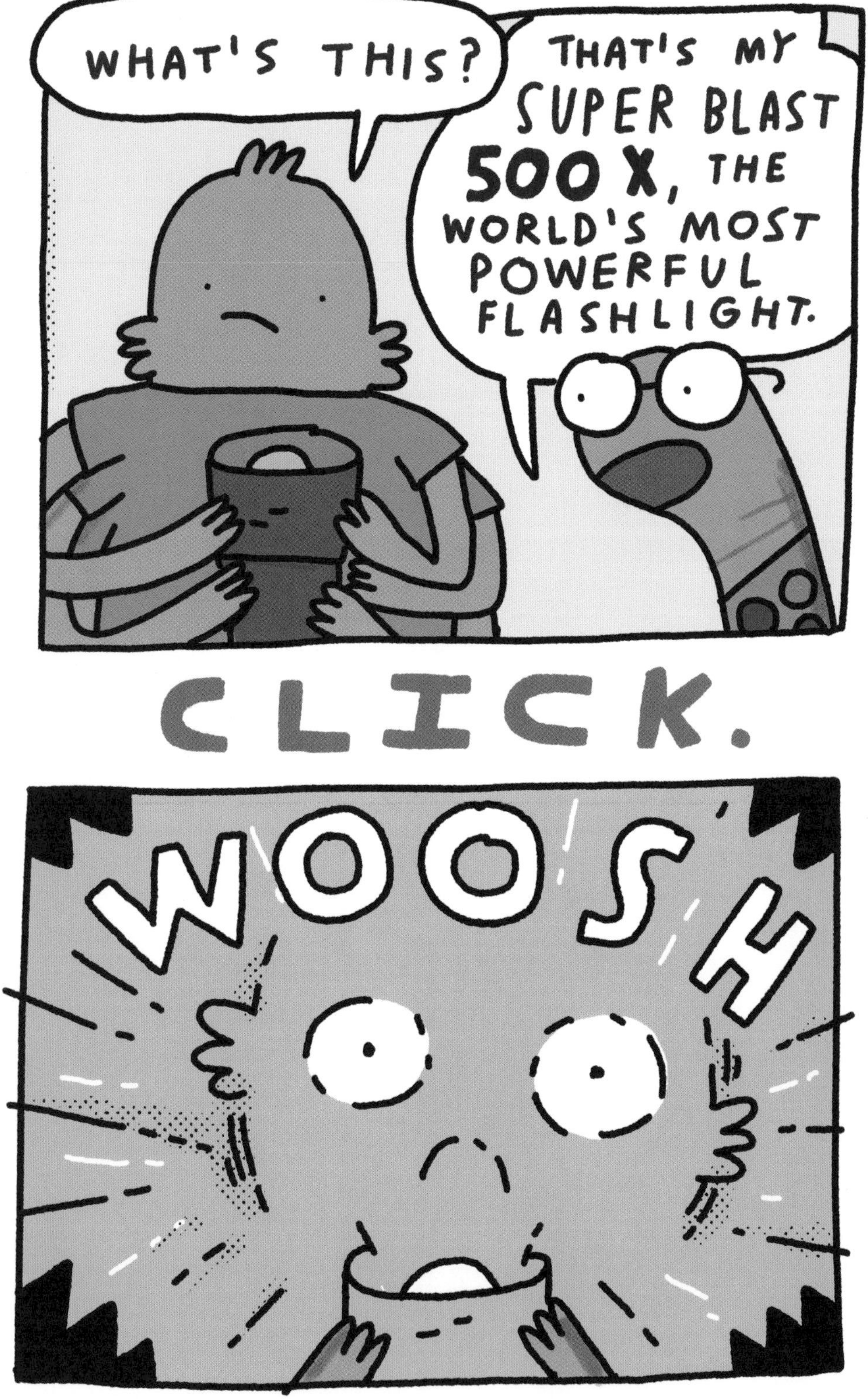
WHAT'S THIS?
THAT'S MY SUPER BLAST 500 X, THE WORLD'S MOST POWERFUL FLASHLIGHT.
CLICK.
WOOSH

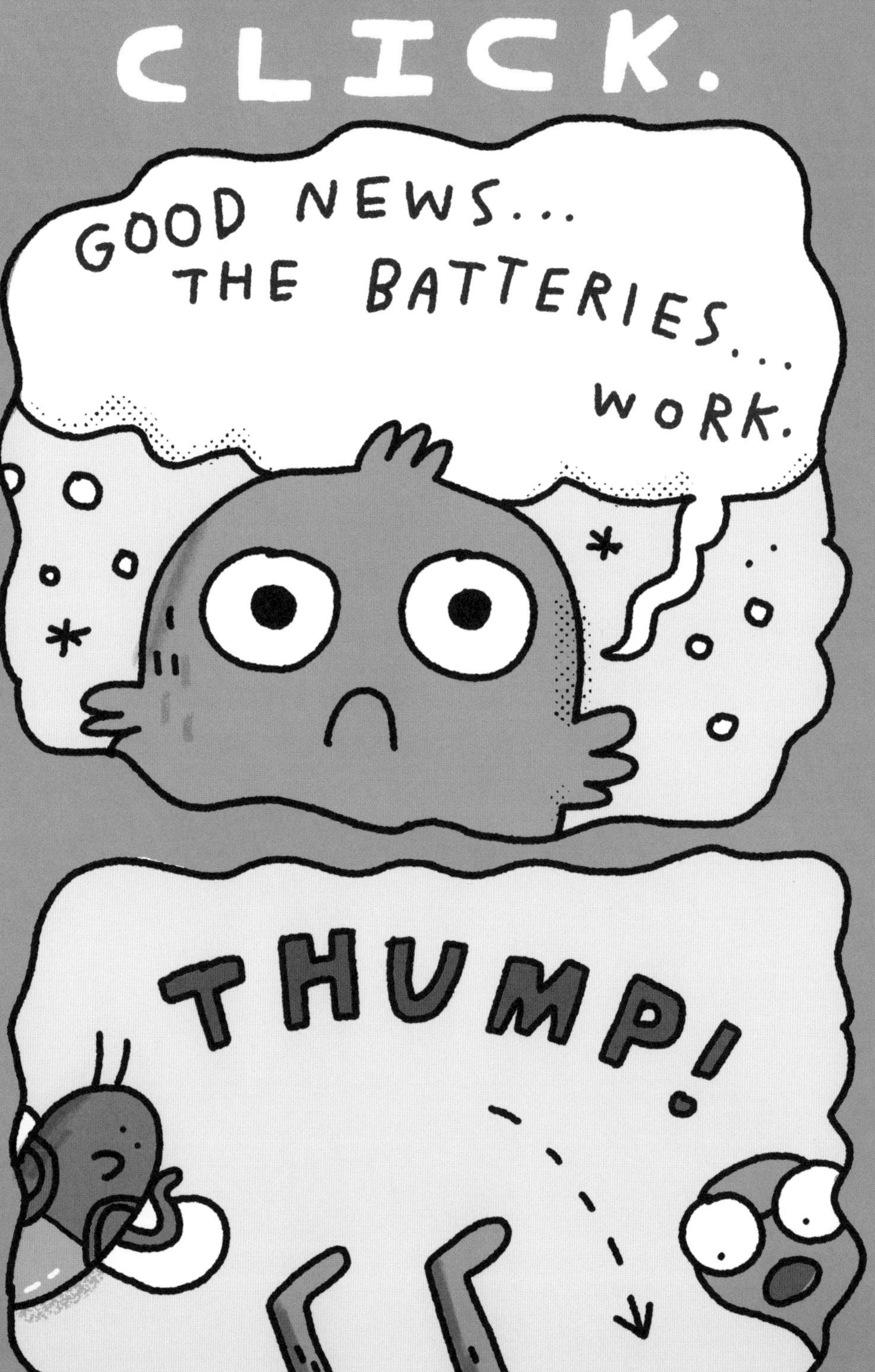
CLICK.
GOOD NEWS...
THE BATTERIES...
WORK.
THUMP!

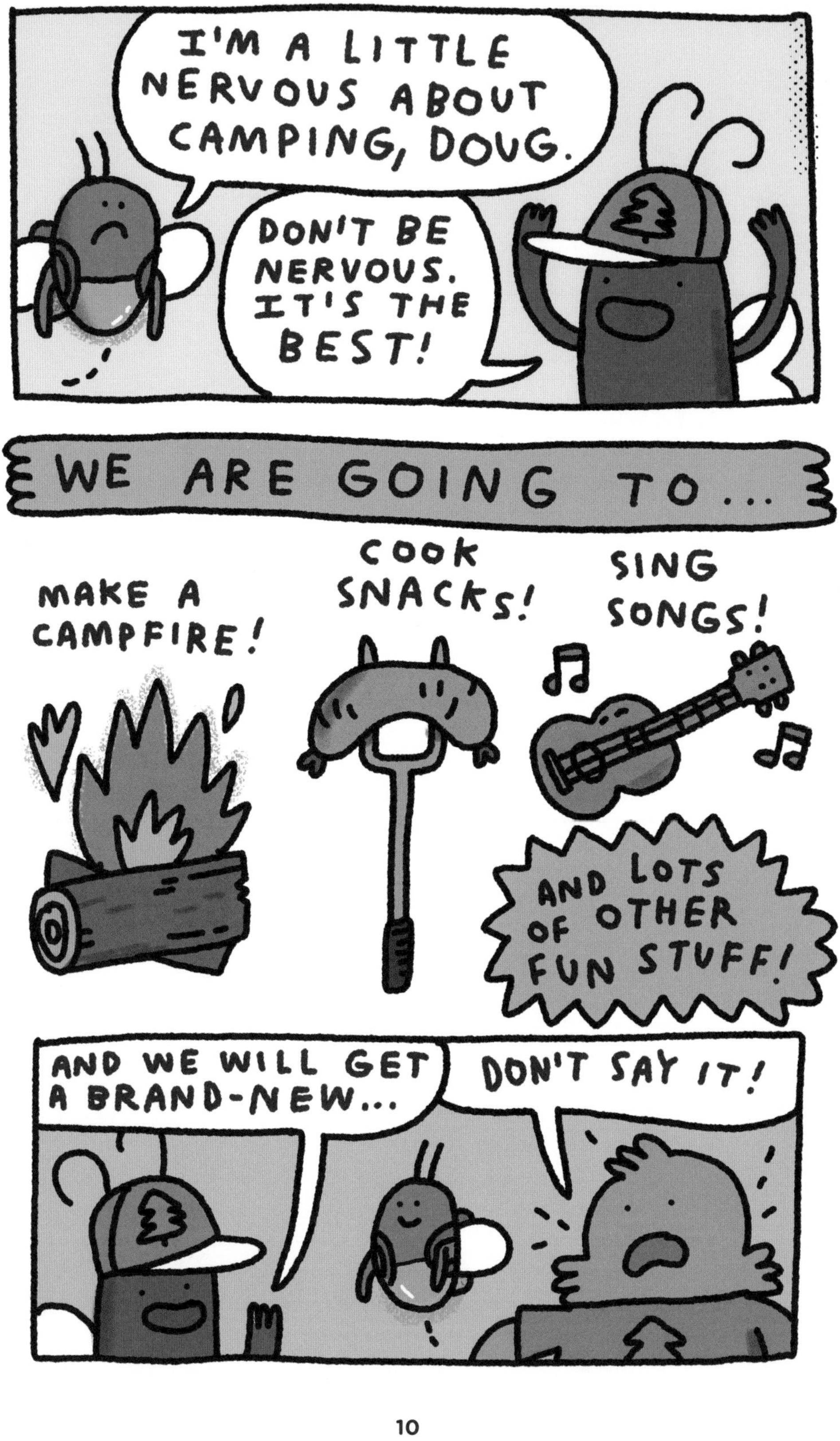
I'M A LITTLE NERVOUS ABOUT CAMPING, DOUG.
DON'T BE NERVOUS. IT'S THE BEST!
WE ARE GOING TO...
MAKE A CAMPFIRE!
COOK SNACKS!
SING SONGS!
AND LOTS OF OTHER FUN STUFF!
AND WE WILL GET A BRAND-NEW...
DON'T SAY IT!

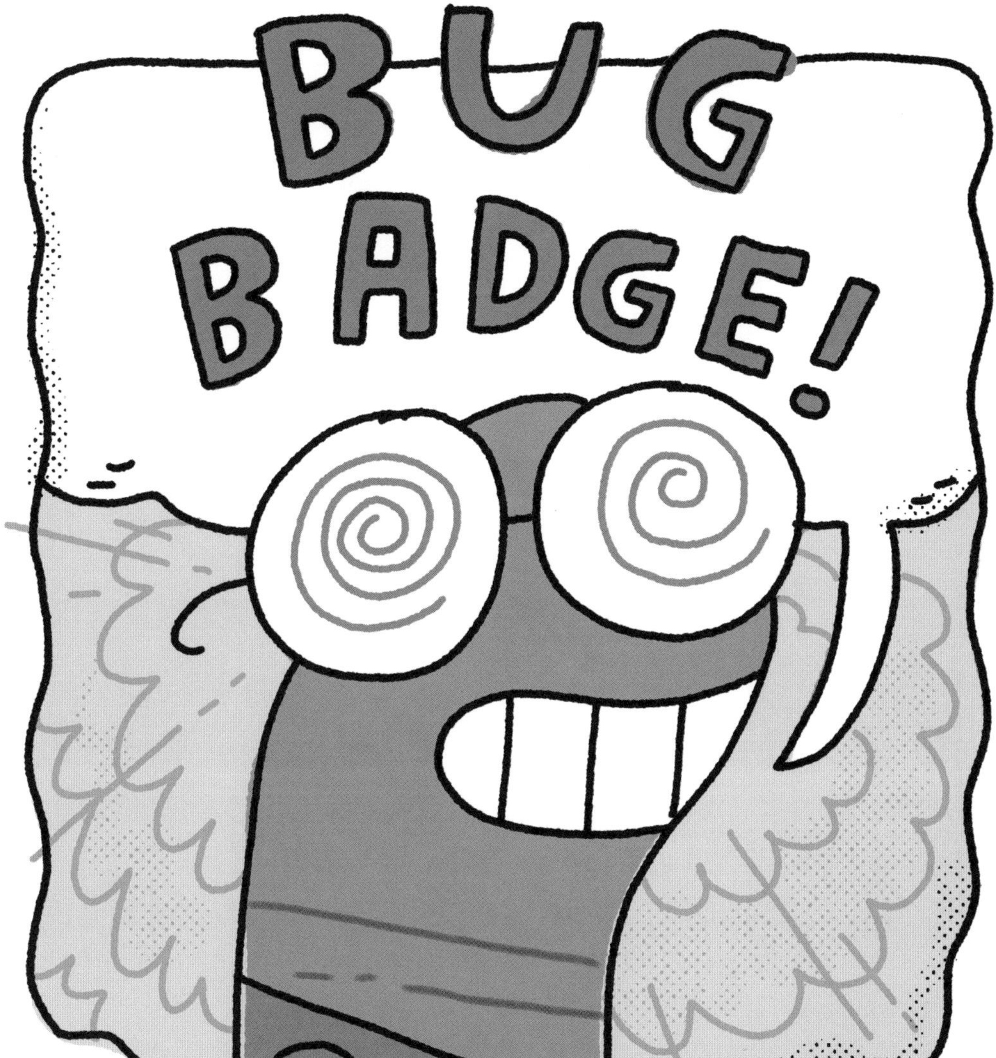
BUG BADGE!

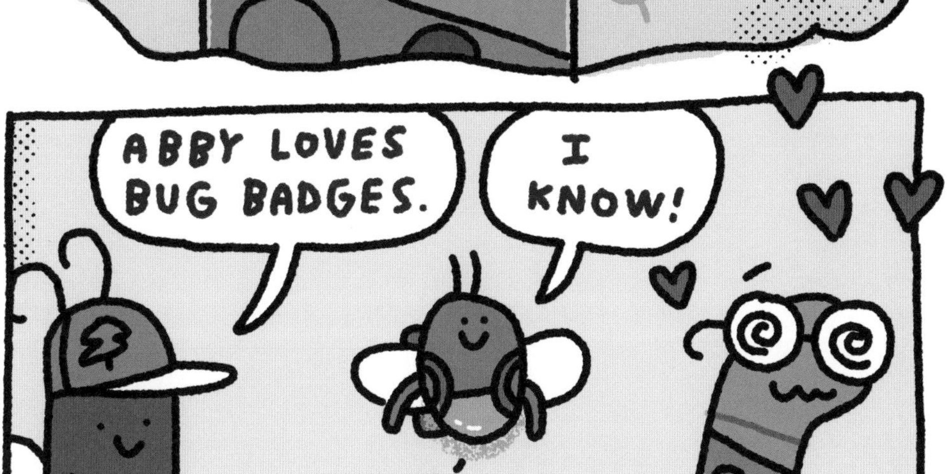
ABBY LOVES BUG BADGES.
I KNOW!

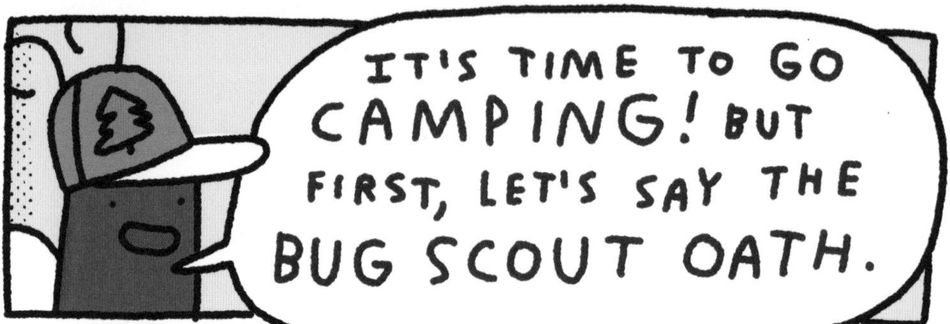
IT'S TIME TO GO CAMPING! BUT FIRST, LET'S SAY THE BUG SCOUT OATH.

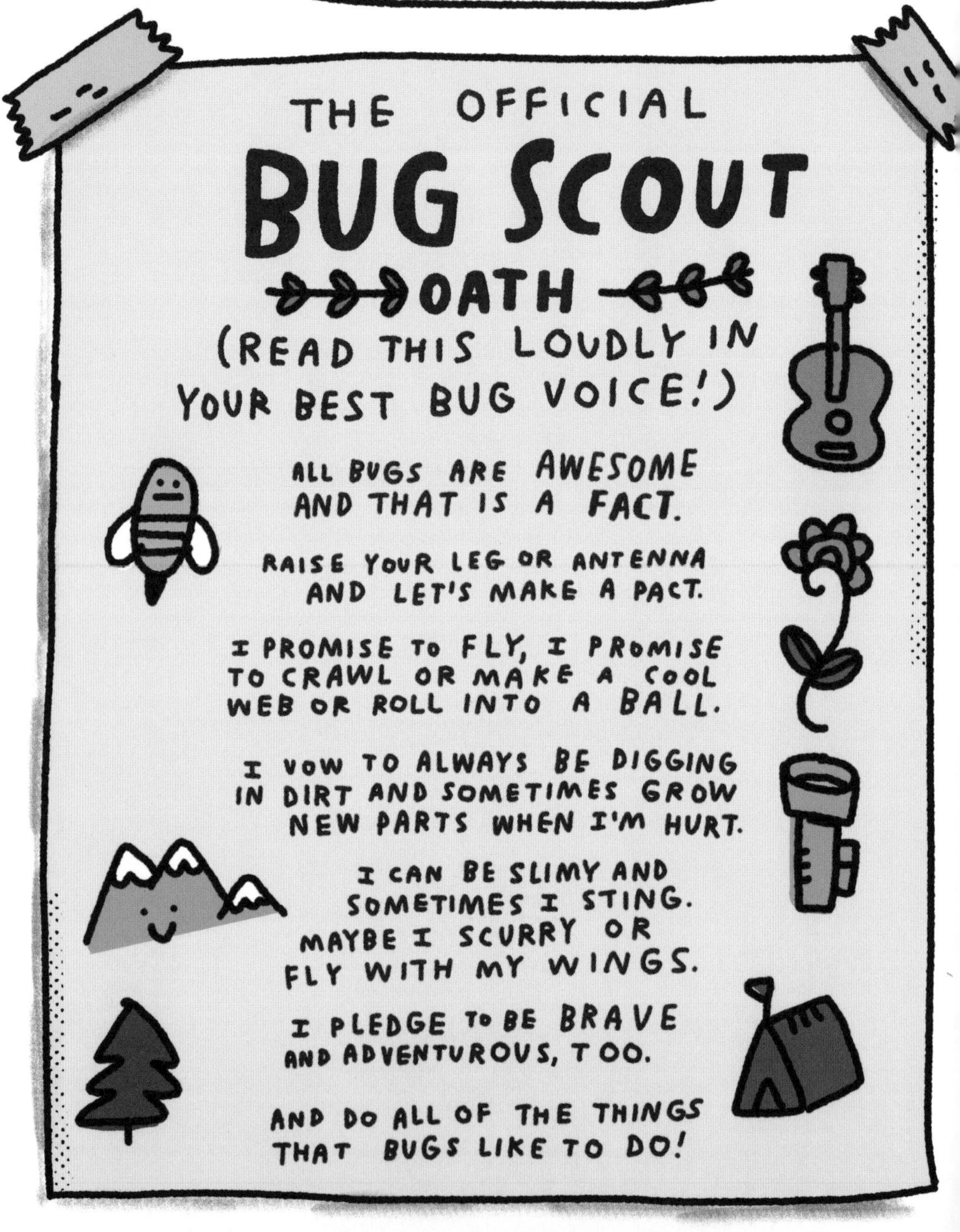
THE OFFICIAL
BUG SCOUT
OATH
(READ THIS LOUDLY IN YOUR BEST BUG VOICE!)
ALL BUGS ARE AWESOME
AND THAT IS A FACT.
RAISE YOUR LEG OR ANTENNA
AND LET'S MAKE A PACT.
I PROMISE TO FLY, I PROMISE
TO CRAWL OR MAKE A COOL
WEB OR ROLL INTO A BALL.
I VOW TO ALWAYS BE DIGGING
IN DIRT AND SOMETIMES GROW
NEW PARTS WHEN I'M HURT.
I CAN BE SLIMY AND
SOMETIMES I STING.
MAYBE I SCURRY OR
FLY WITH MY WINGS.
I PLEDGE TO BE BRAVE
AND ADVENTUROUS, TOO.
AND DO ALL OF THE THINGS
THAT BUGS LIKE TO DO!

CHAPTER 2

THE WOODS

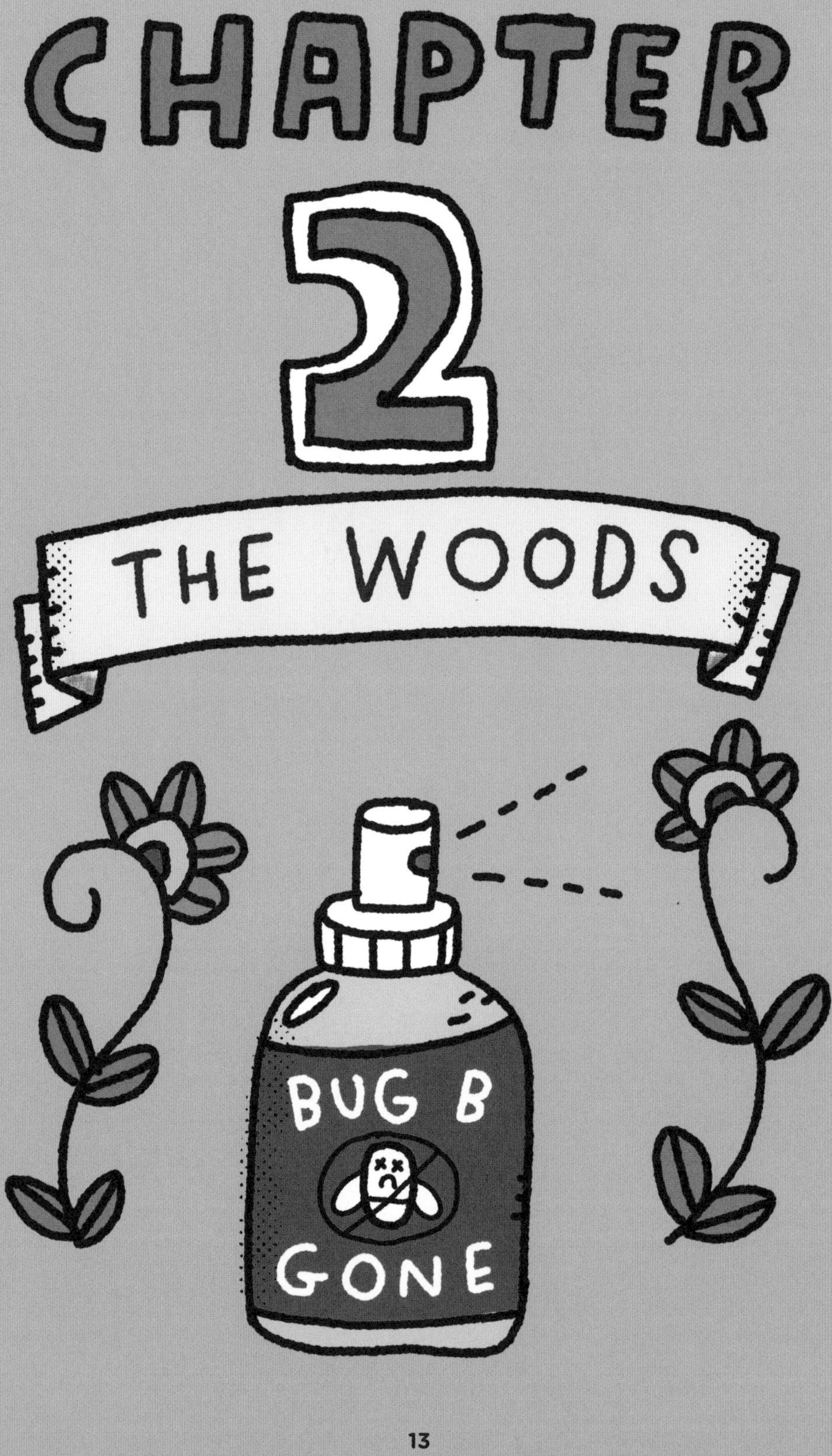
BUG B
GONE

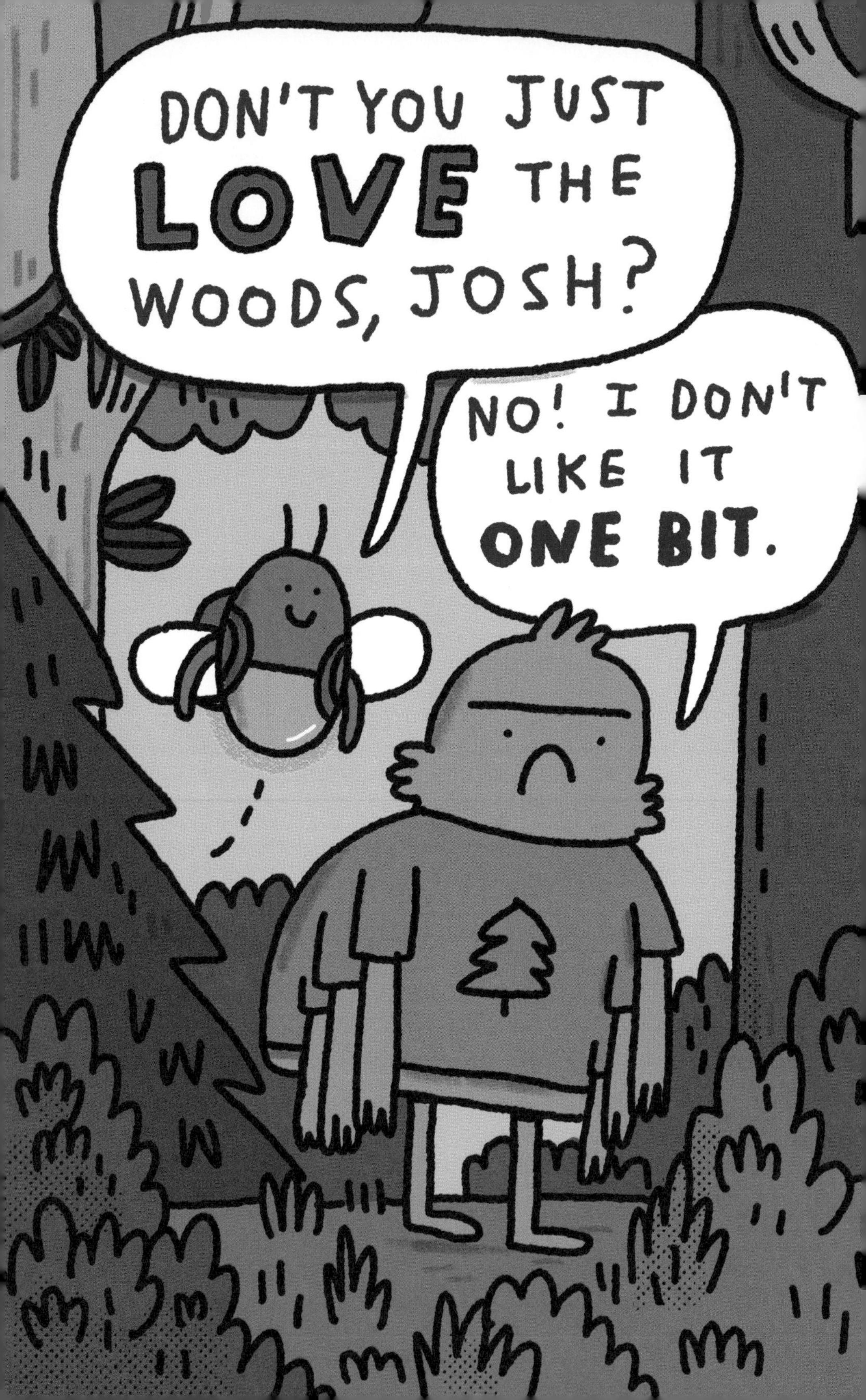
DON'T YOU JUST LOVE THE WOODS, JOSH?
NO! I DON'T LIKE IT ONE BIT.

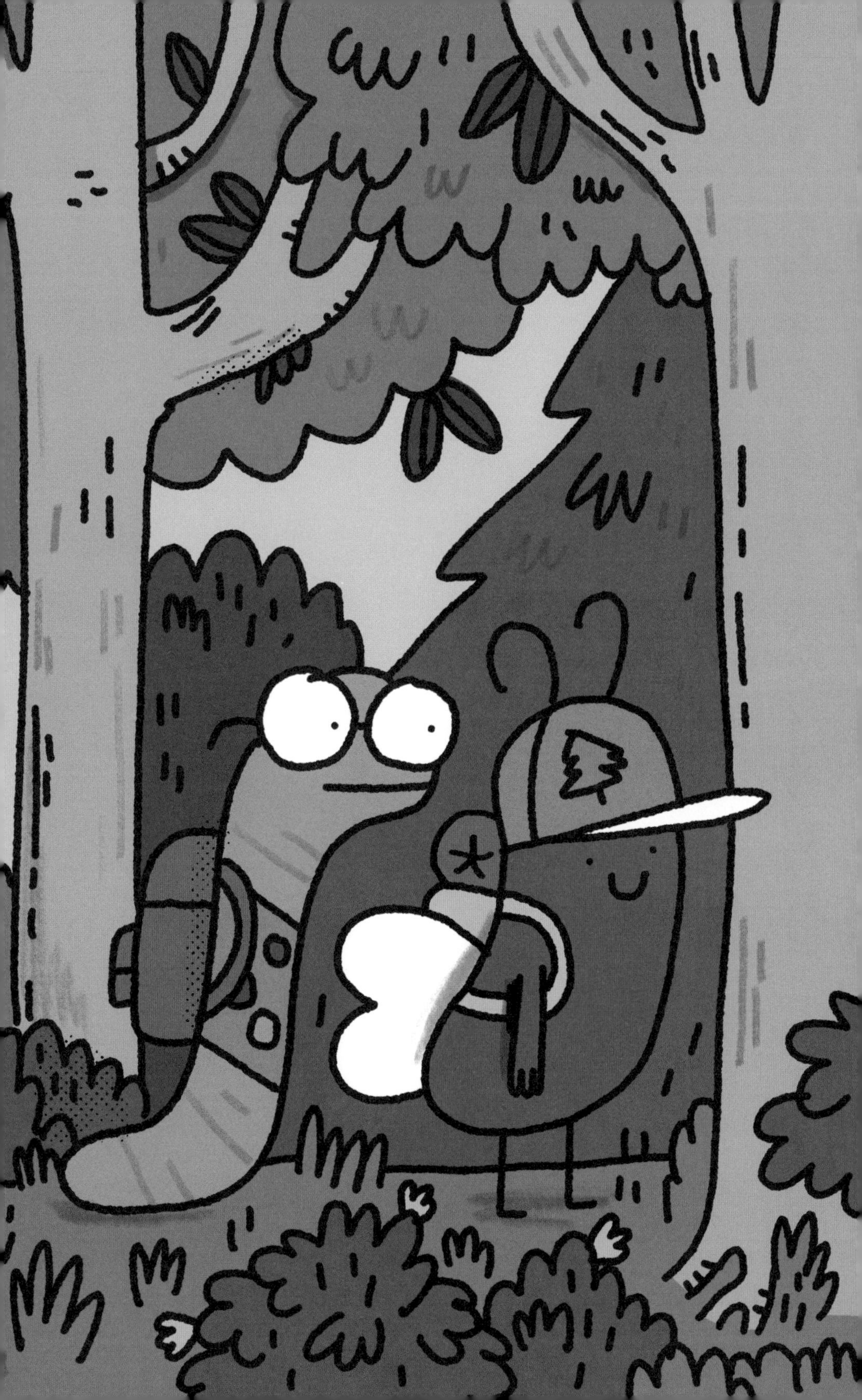

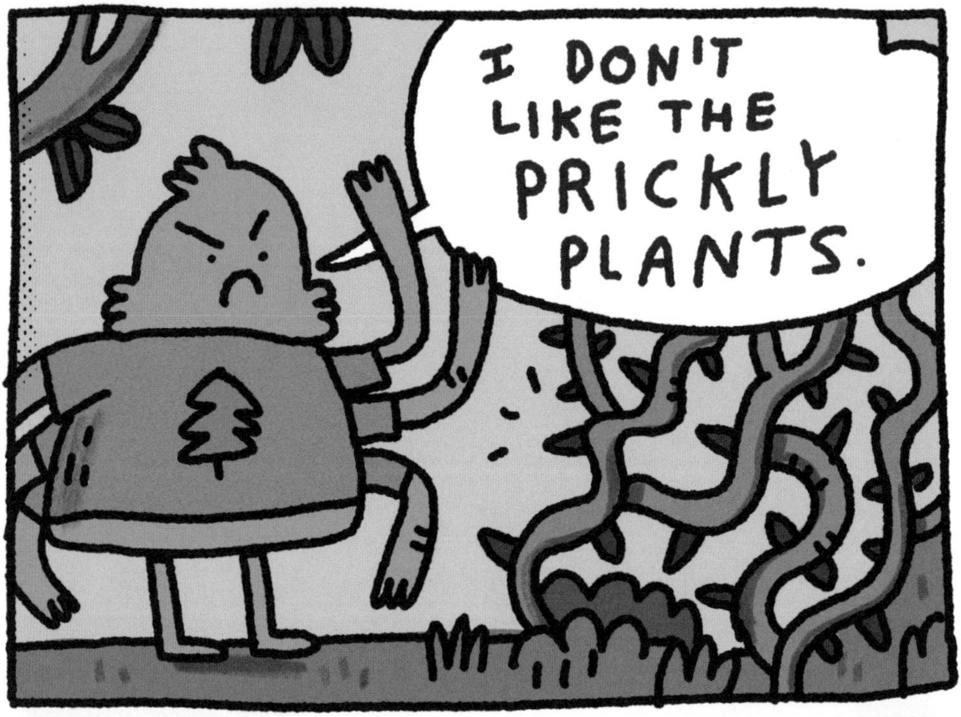
I DON'T LIKE THE PRICKLY PLANTS.

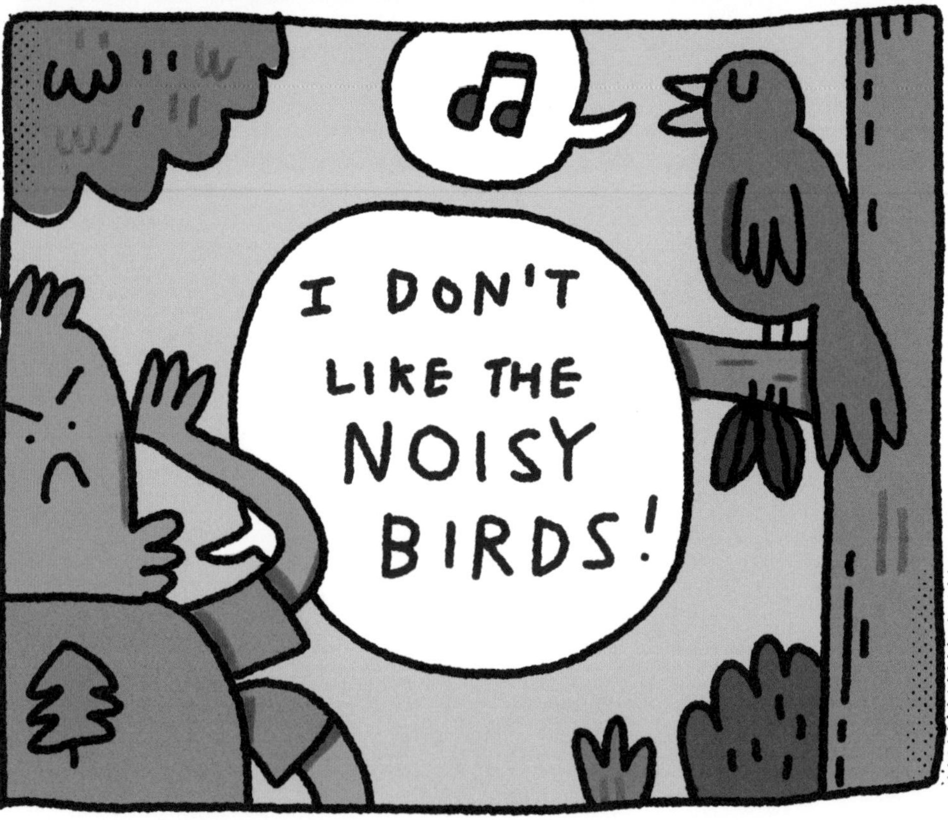
♫
I DON'T LIKE THE NOISY BIRDS!

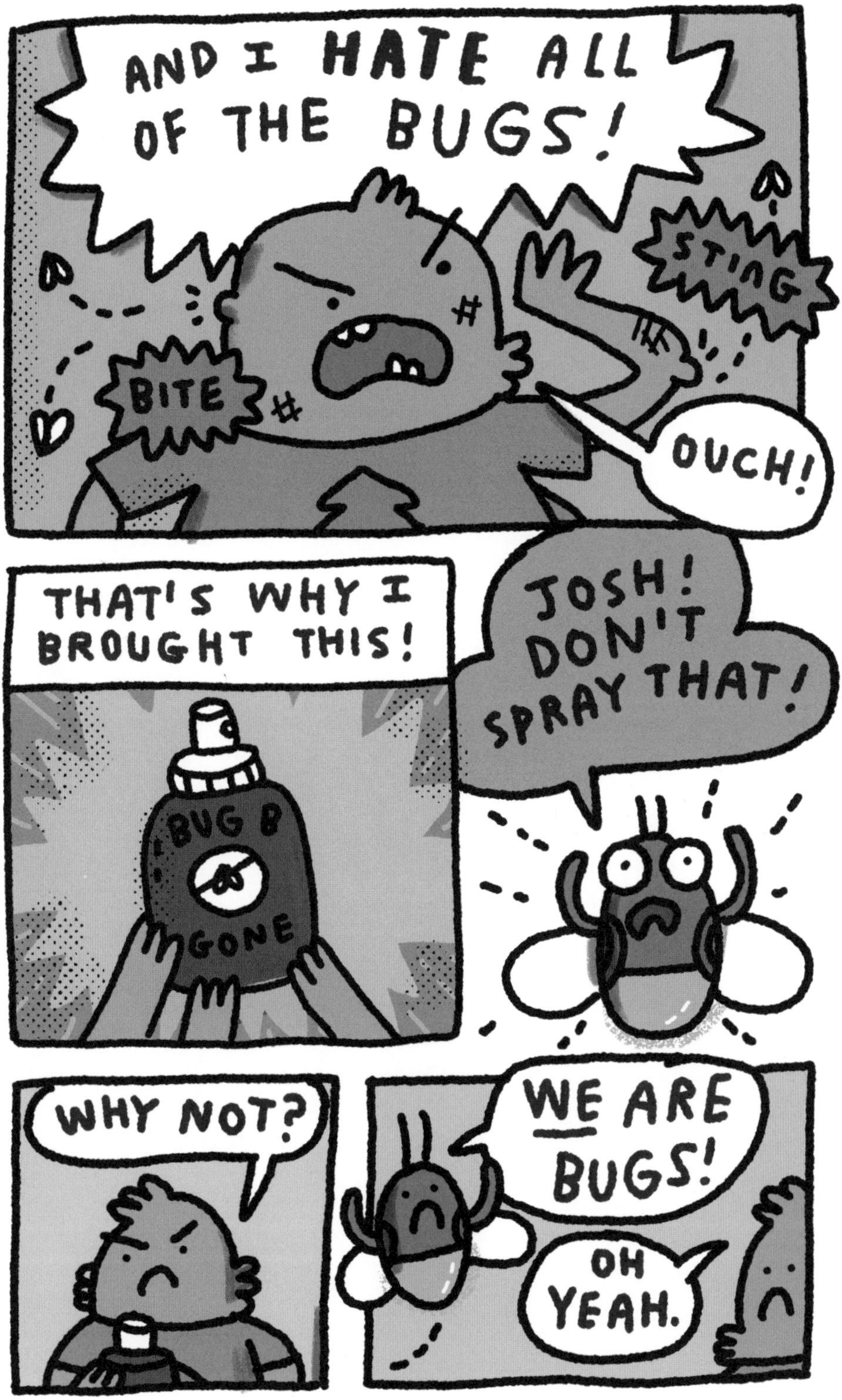
AND I HATE ALL OF THE BUGS!
BITE
STING
OUCH!
THAT'S WHY I BROUGHT THIS!
BUG B GONE
JOSH! DON'T SPRAY THAT!
WHY NOT?
WE ARE BUGS!
OH YEAH.

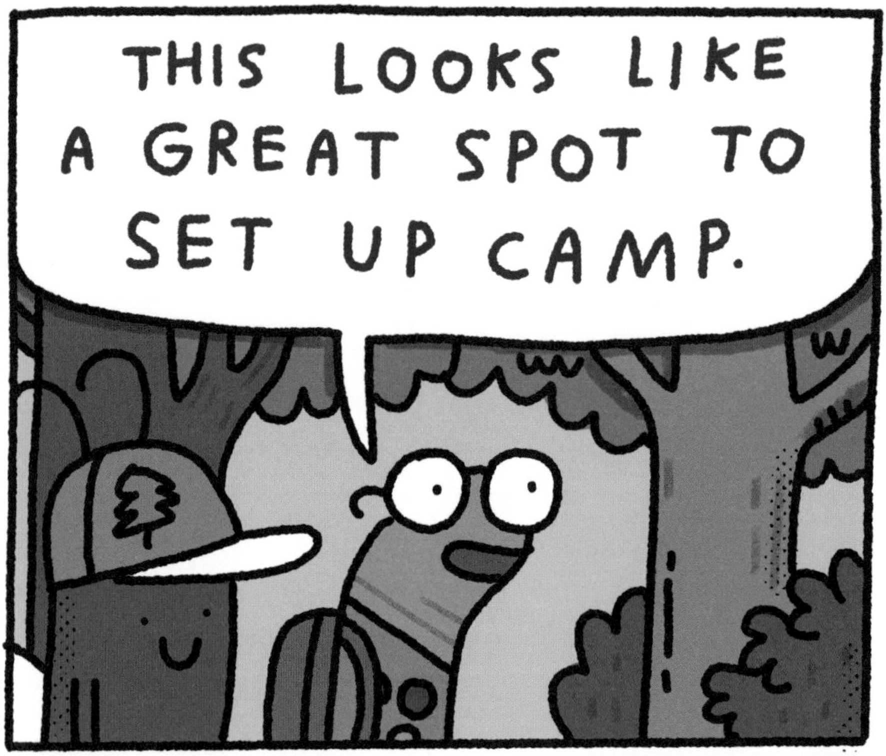
THIS LOOKS LIKE A GREAT SPOT TO SET UP CAMP.

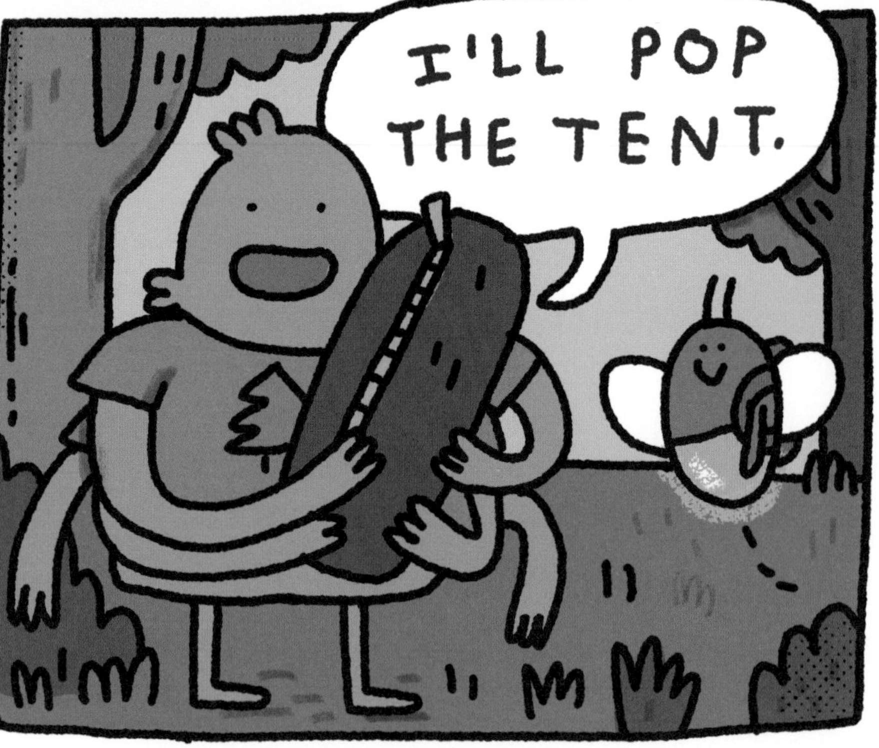
I'LL POP THE TENT.

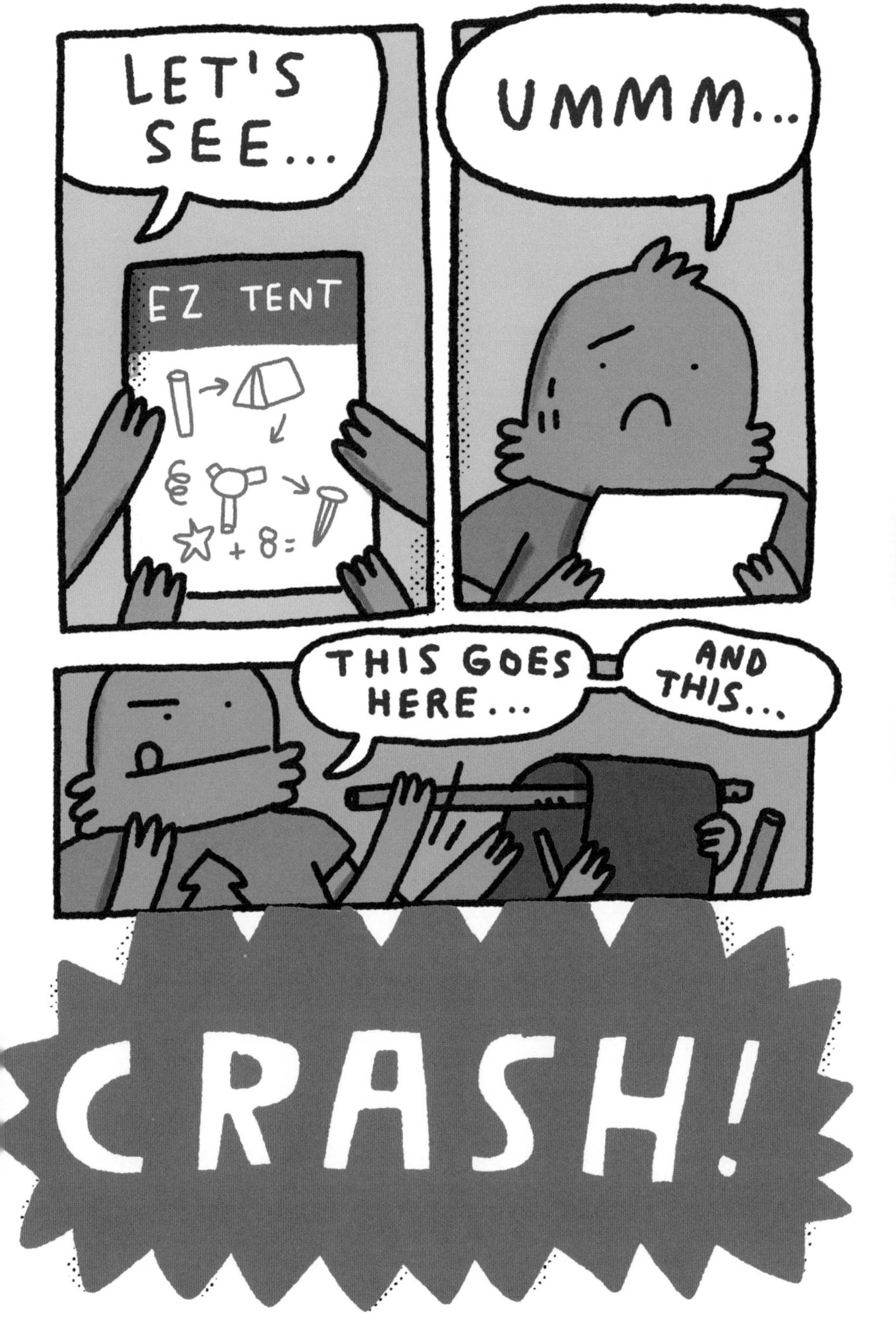
LET'S SEE...
EZ TENT
+ 8 =
UMMM...
THIS GOES HERE...
AND THIS...
CRASH!

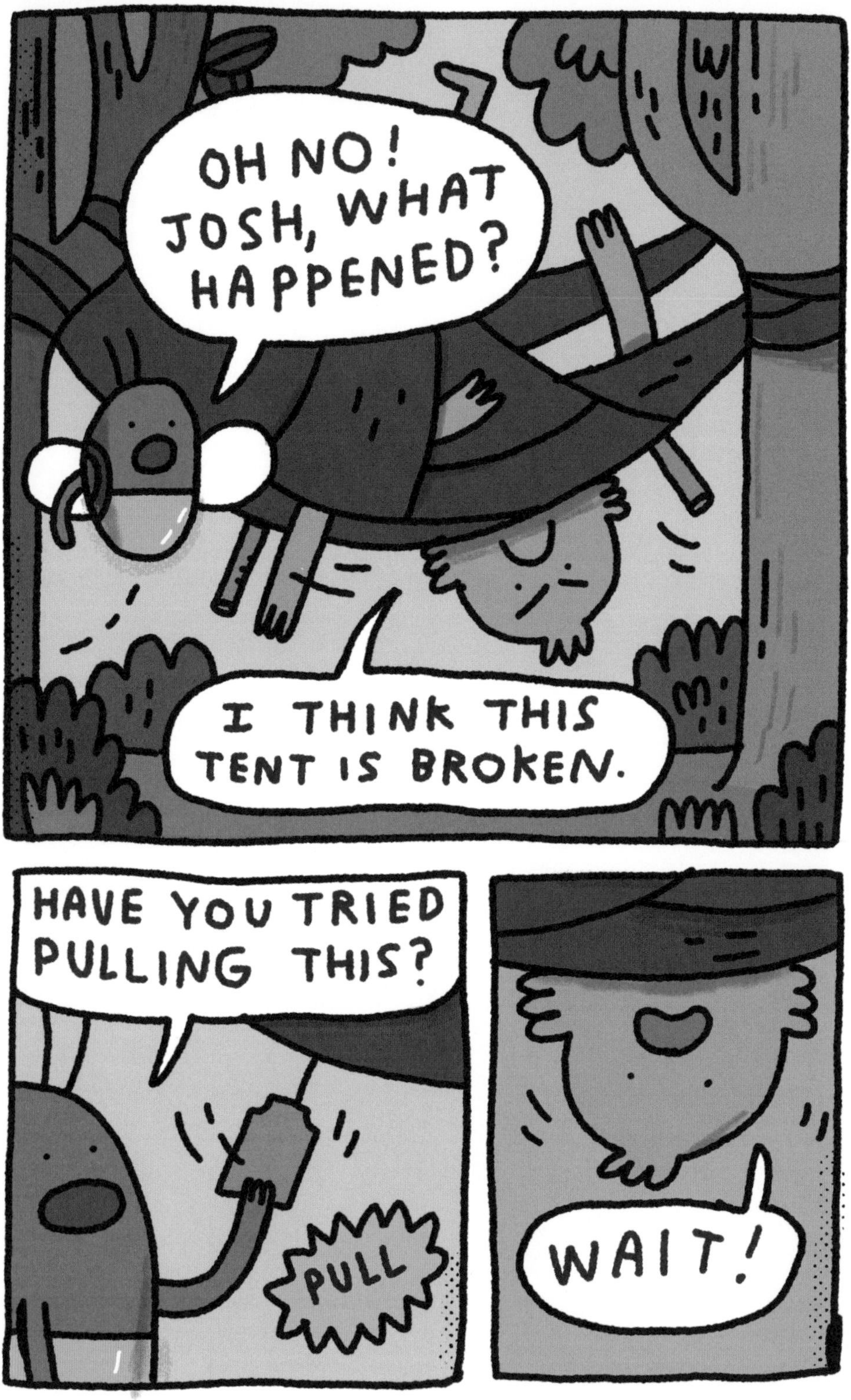
OH NO! JOSH, WHAT HAPPENED?
I THINK THIS TENT IS BROKEN.
HAVE YOU TRIED PULLING THIS?
PULL
WAIT!

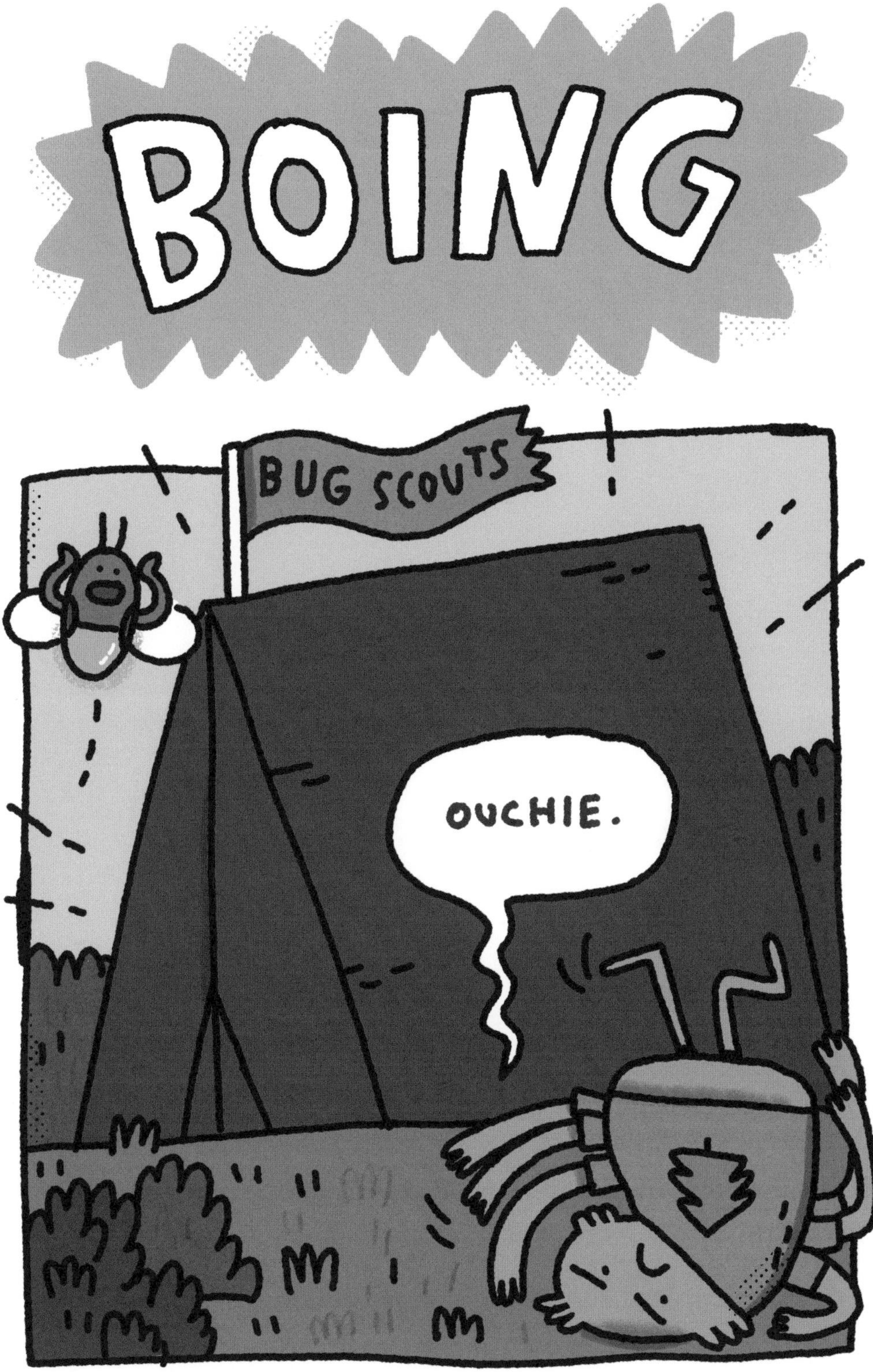
BOING
BUG SCOUTS
OUCHIE.

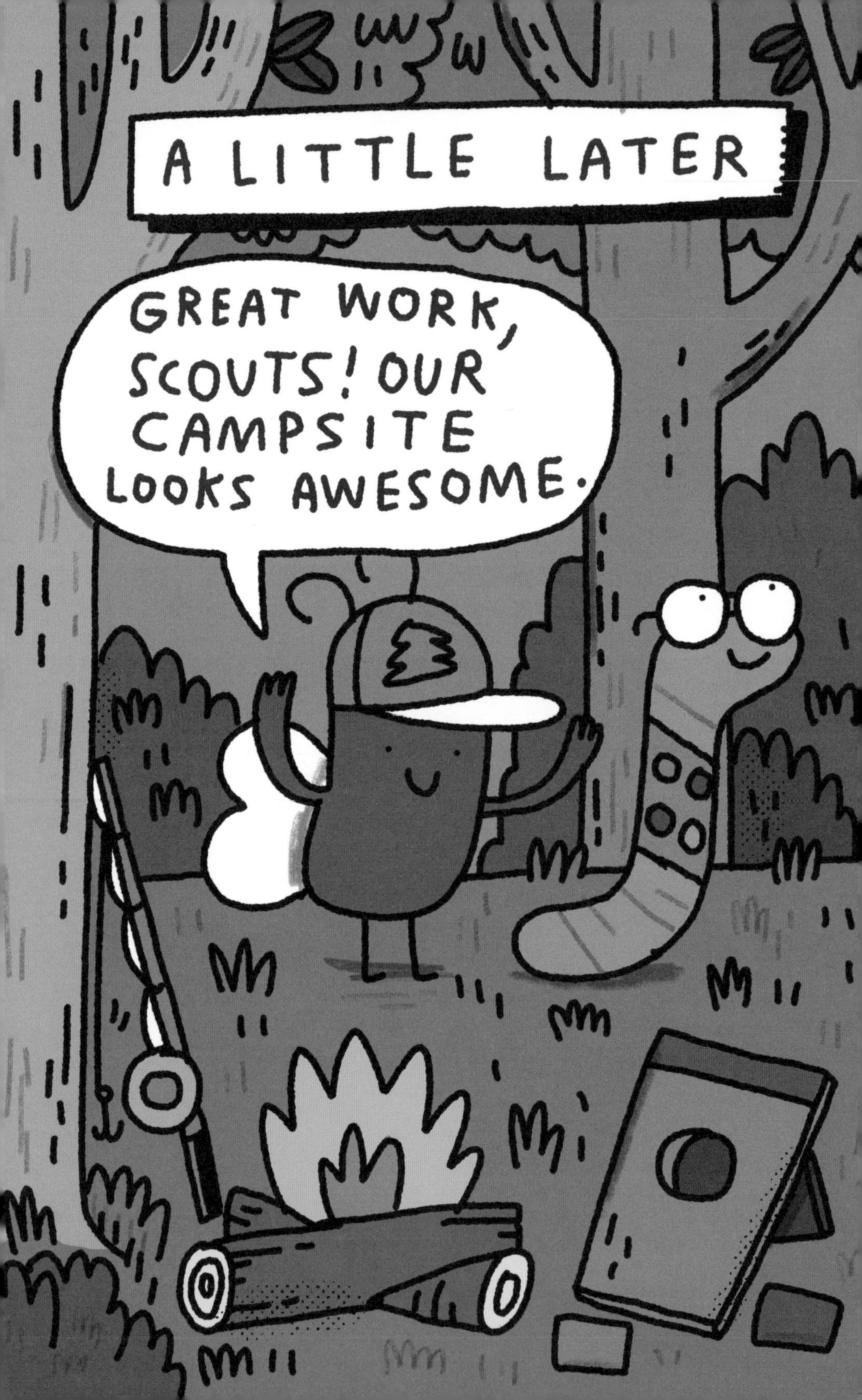
A LITTLE LATER
GREAT WORK, SCOUTS! OUR CAMPSITE LOOKS AWESOME.

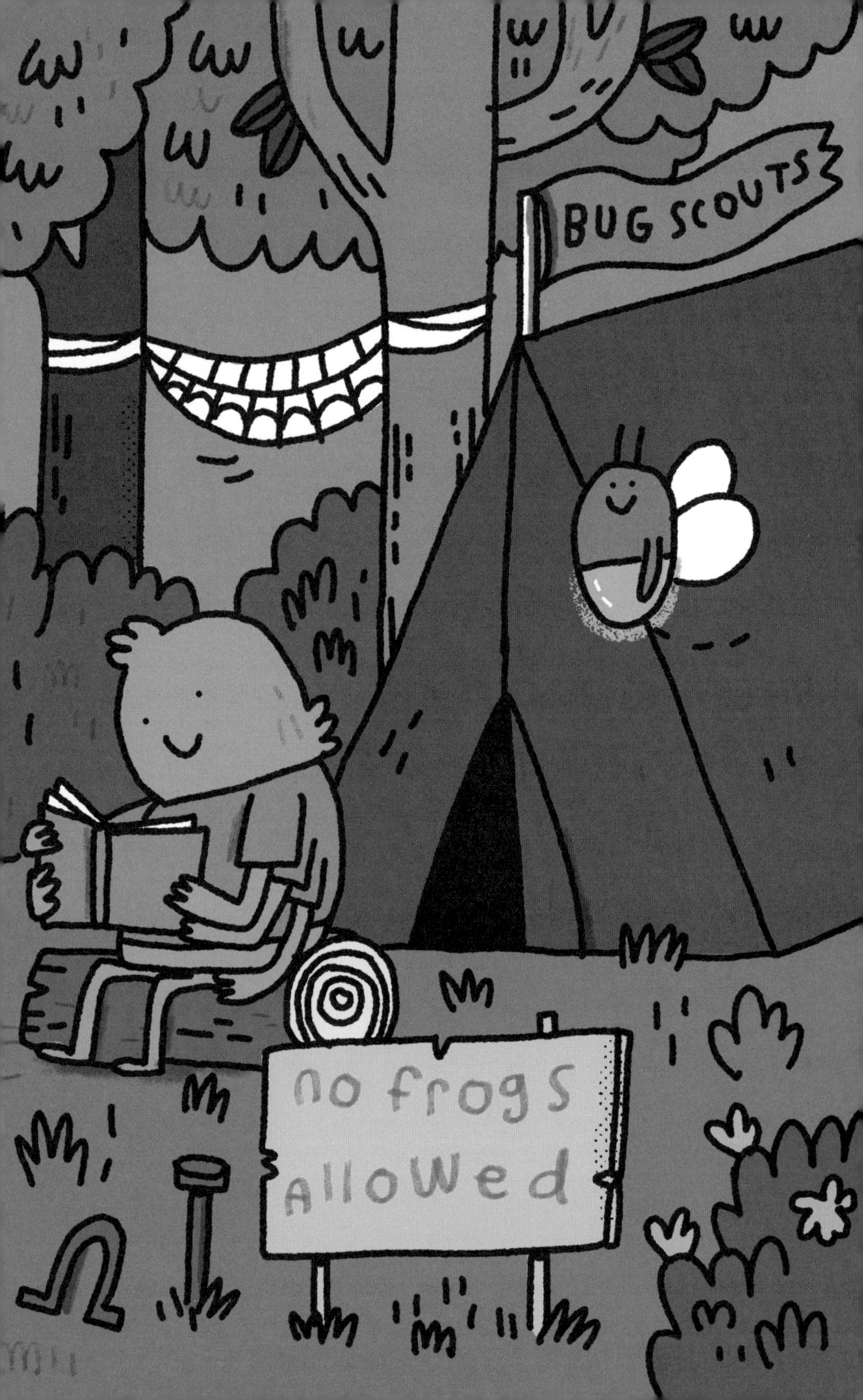
BUG SCOUTS
no frogs allowed

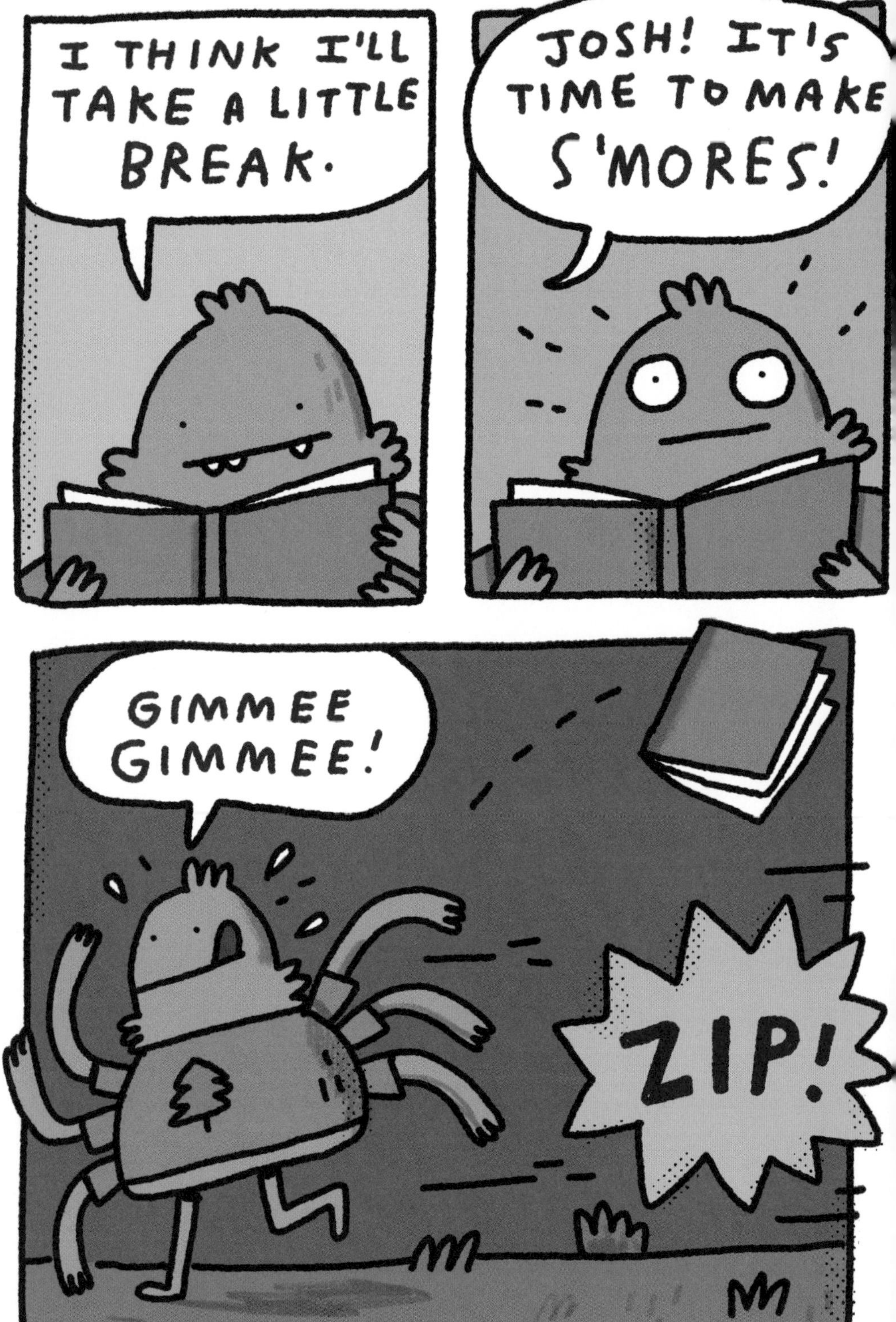
I THINK I'LL TAKE A LITTLE BREAK.
JOSH! IT'S TIME TO MAKE S'MORES!
GIMMEE GIMMEE!
ZIP!

CHAPTER 3

MAKING S'MORES

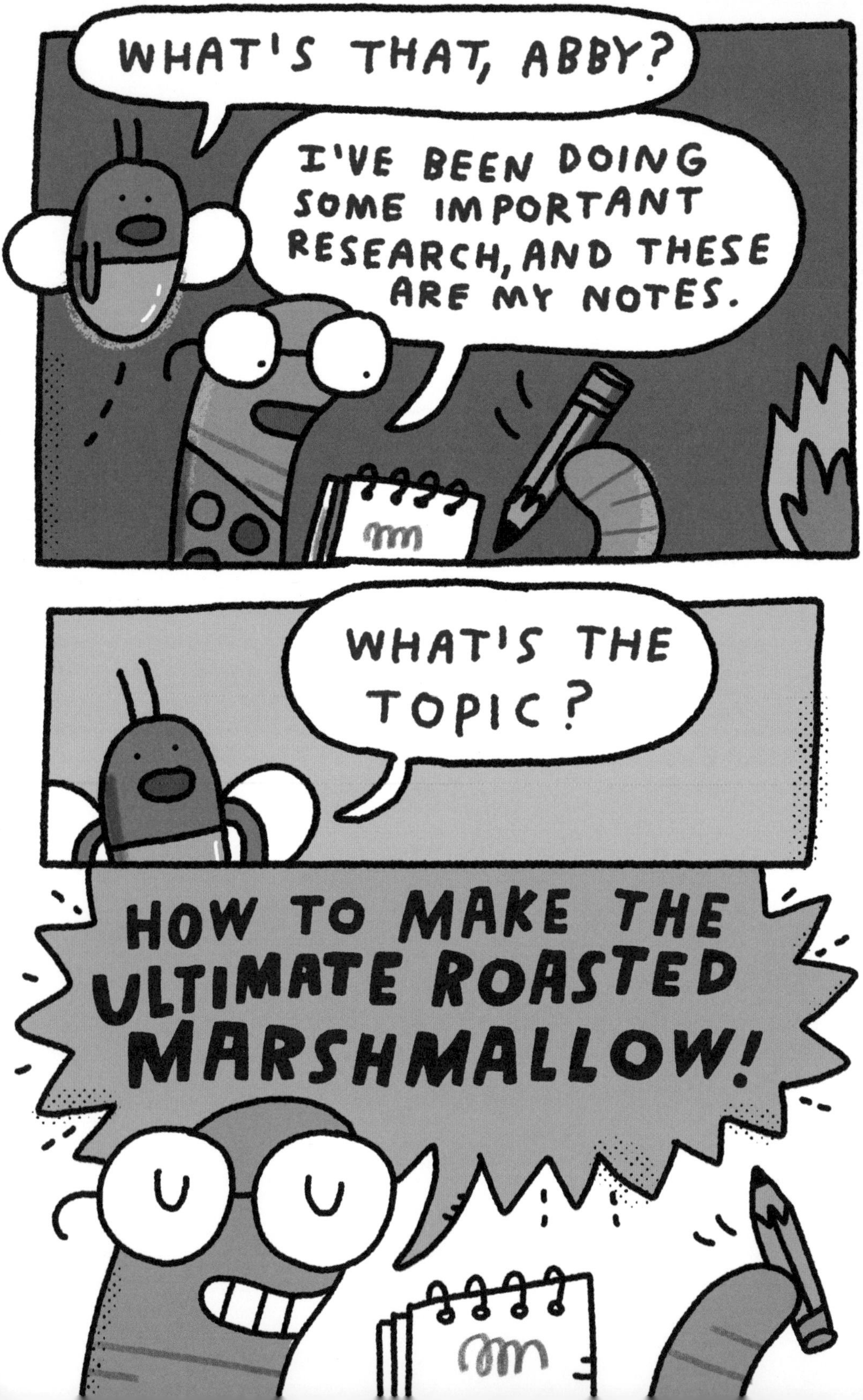
WHAT'S THAT, ABBY?
I'VE BEEN DOING SOME IMPORTANT RESEARCH, AND THESE ARE MY NOTES.
WHAT'S THE TOPIC?
HOW TO MAKE THE ULTIMATE ROASTED MARSHMALLOW!

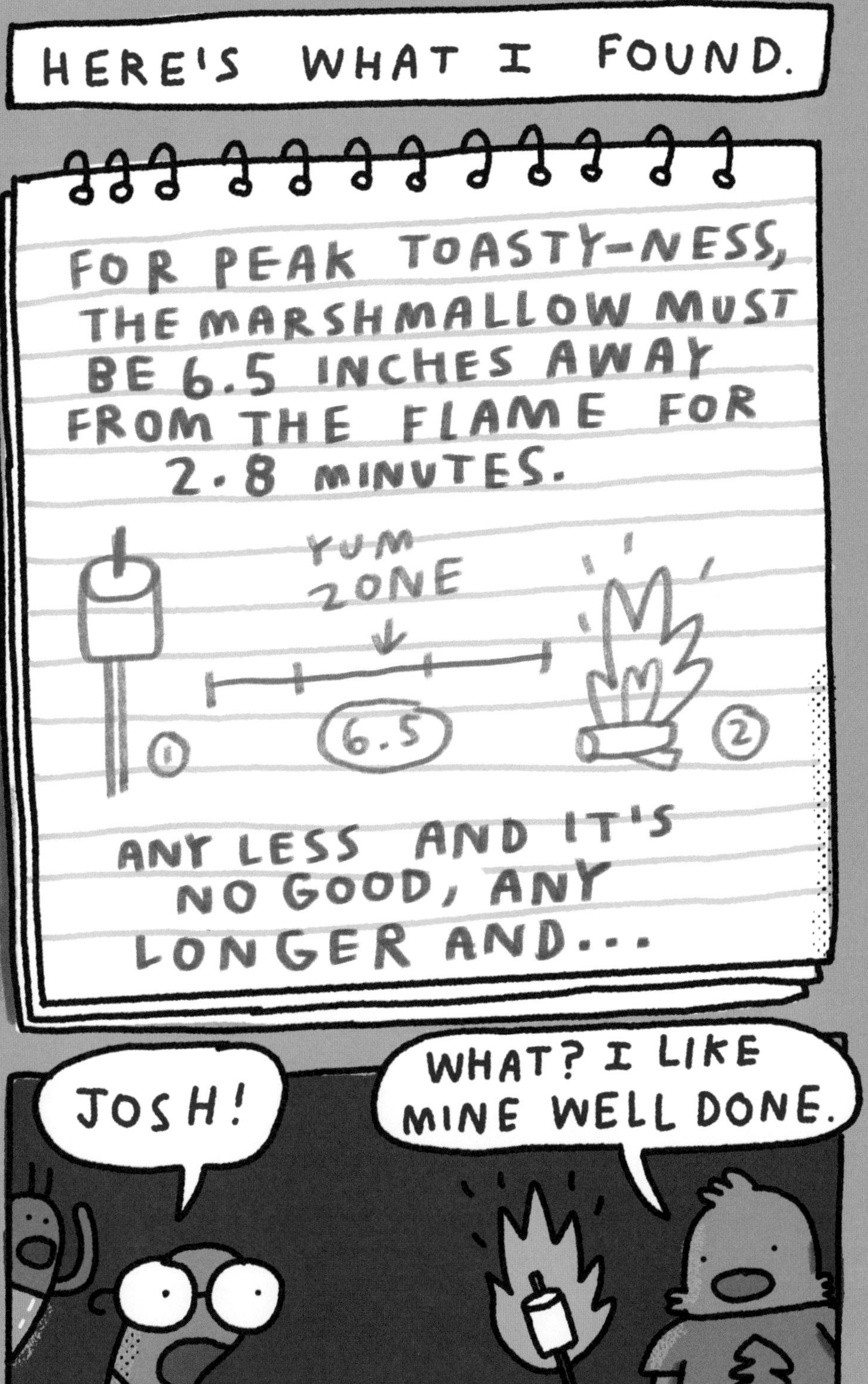
HERE'S WHAT I FOUND.
FOR PEAK TOASTY-NESS, THE MARSHMALLOW MUST BE 6.5 INCHES AWAY FROM THE FLAME FOR 2.8 MINUTES.
YUM ZONE
1
6.5
2
ANY LESS AND IT'S NO GOOD, ANY LONGER AND...
JOSH!
WHAT? I LIKE MINE WELL DONE.

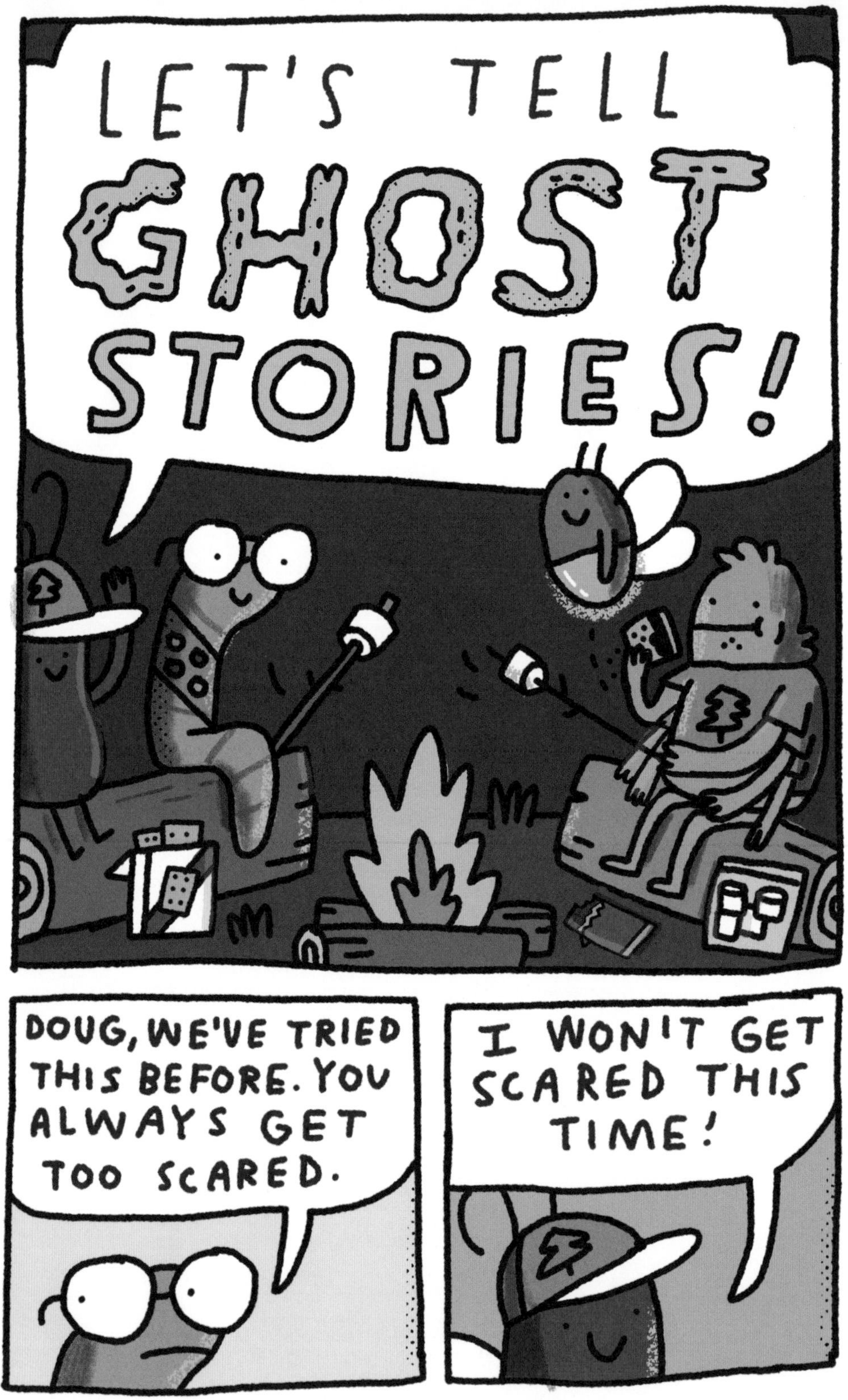
LET'S TELL GHOST STORIES!
DOUG, WE'VE TRIED THIS BEFORE. YOU ALWAYS GET TOO SCARED.
I WON'T GET SCARED THIS TIME!

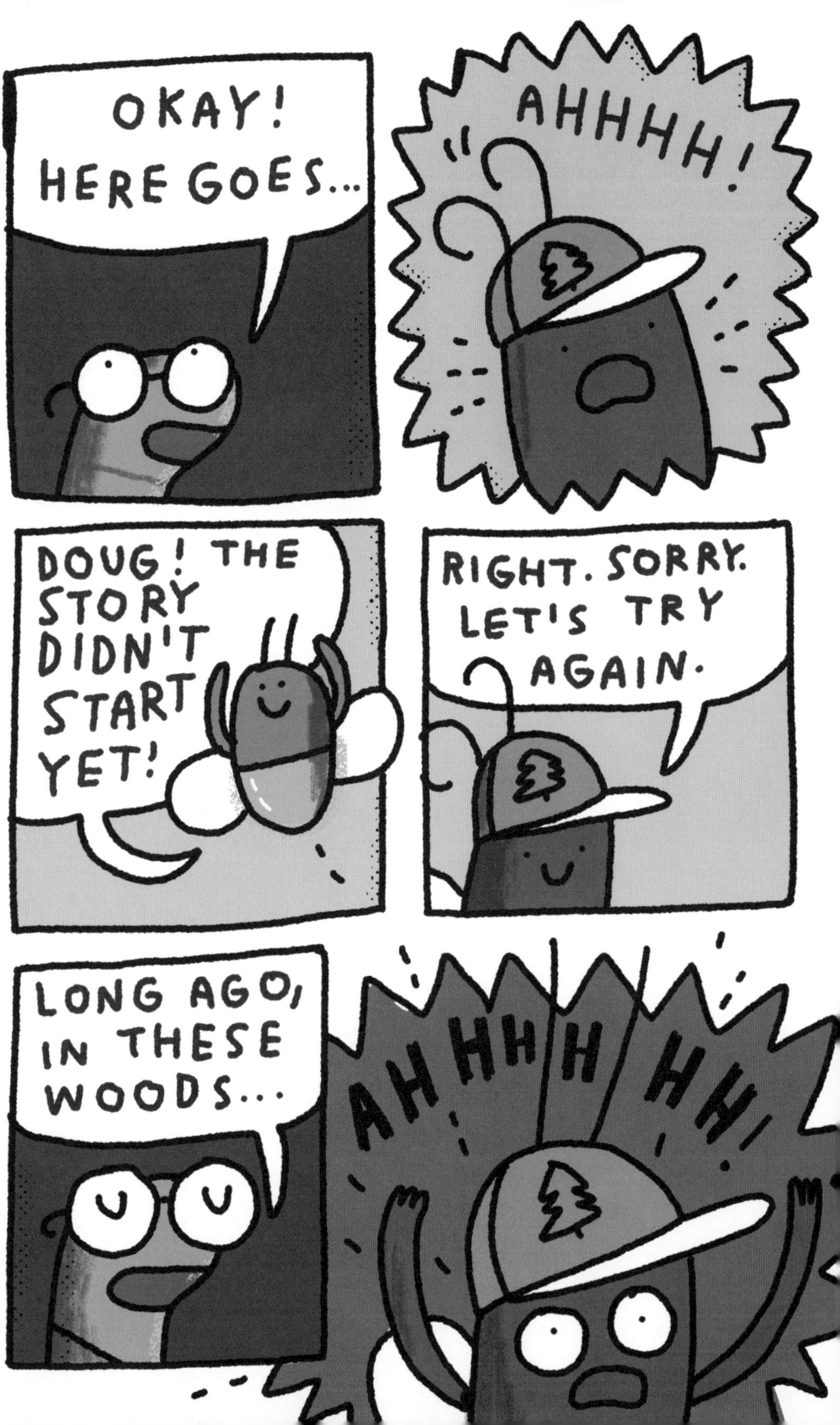
OKAY! HERE GOES...
AHHHHH!
DOUG! THE STORY DIDN'T START YET!
RIGHT. SORRY. LET'S TRY AGAIN.
LONG AGO, IN THESE WOODS...
AHHHHHH!

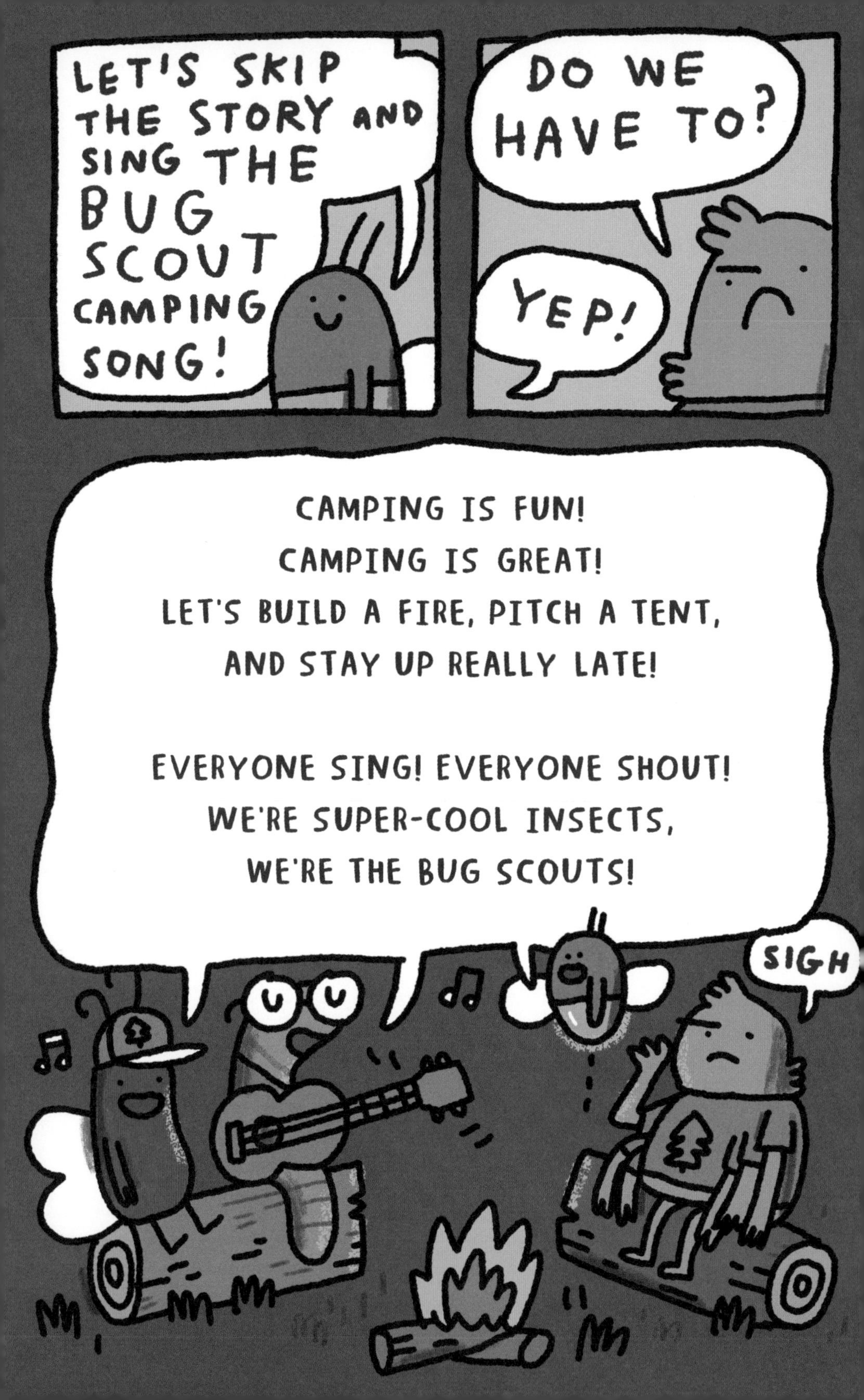
LET'S SKIP THE STORY AND SING THE BUG SCOUT CAMPING SONG!
DO WE HAVE TO?
YEP!
CAMPING IS FUN!
CAMPING IS GREAT!
LET'S BUILD A FIRE, PITCH A TENT,
AND STAY UP REALLY LATE!

EVERYONE SING! EVERYONE SHOUT!
WE'RE SUPER-COOL INSECTS,
WE'RE THE BUG SCOUTS!
SIGH

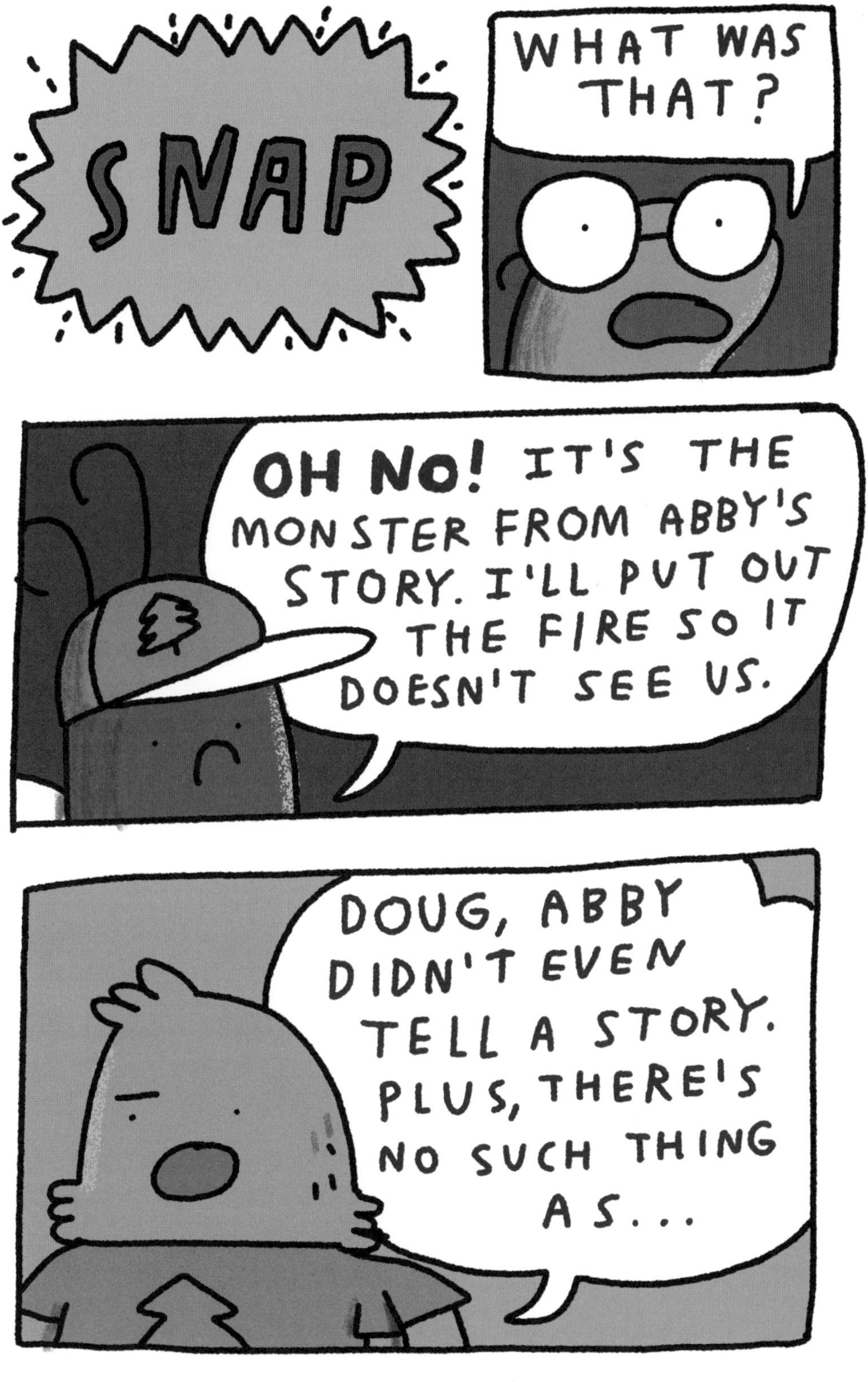
SNAP
WHAT WAS THAT?
OH NO! IT'S THE MONSTER FROM ABBY'S STORY. I'LL PUT OUT THE FIRE SO IT DOESN'T SEE US.
DOUG, ABBY DIDN'T EVEN TELL A STORY. PLUS, THERE'S NO SUCH THING AS...

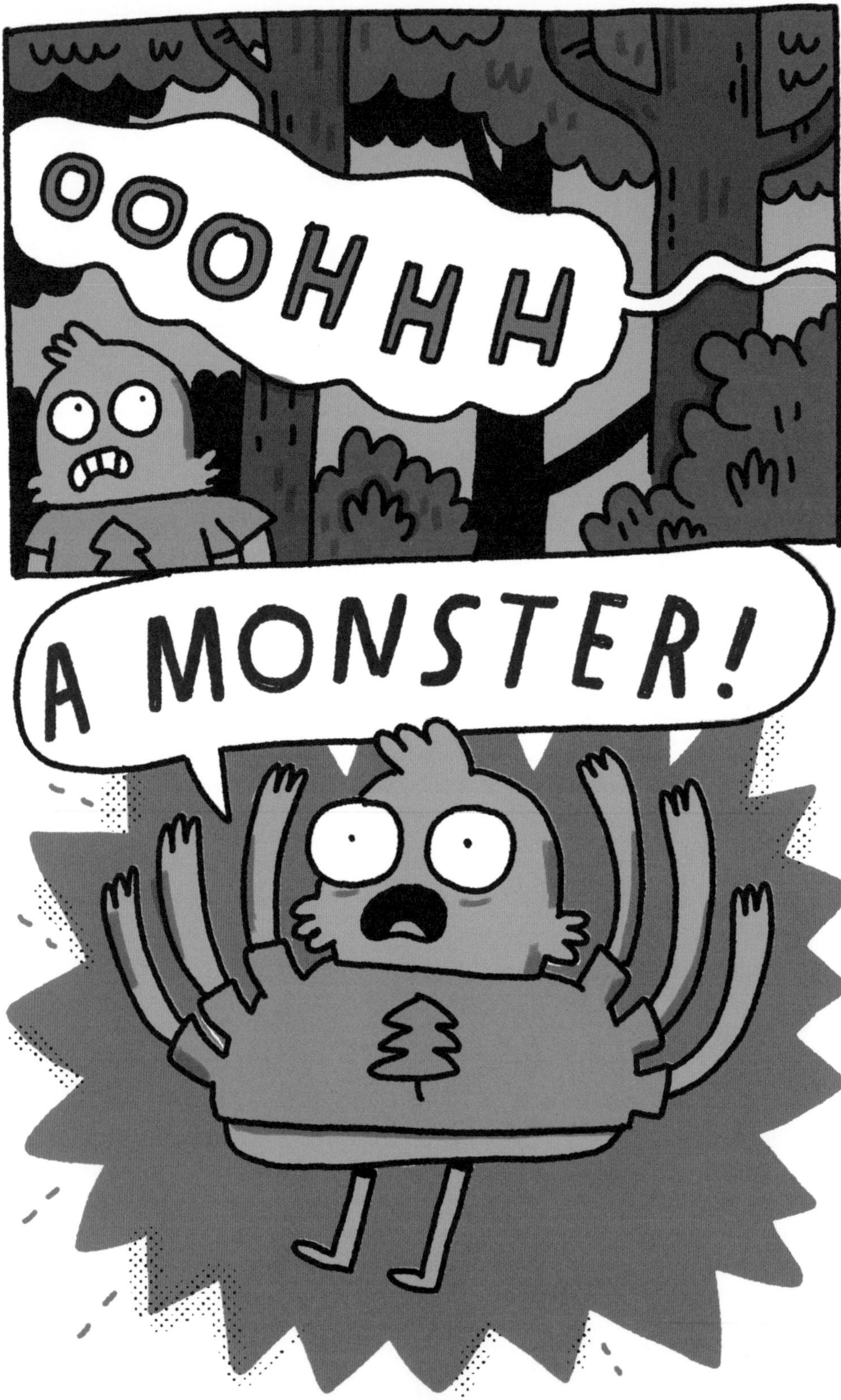
OOOHHHH
A MONSTER!

CHAPTER 4

THE MONSTER

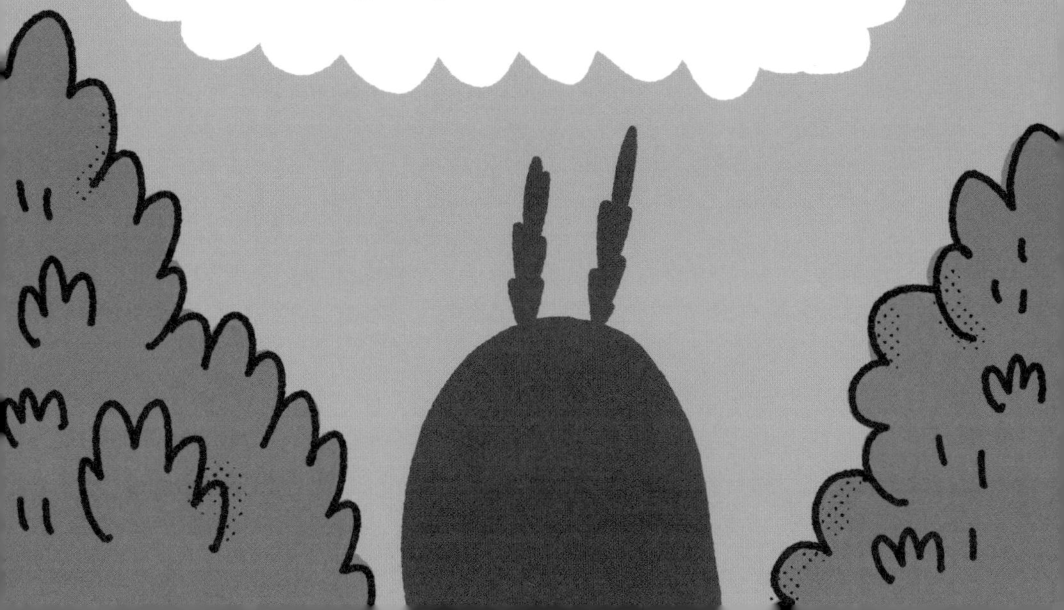

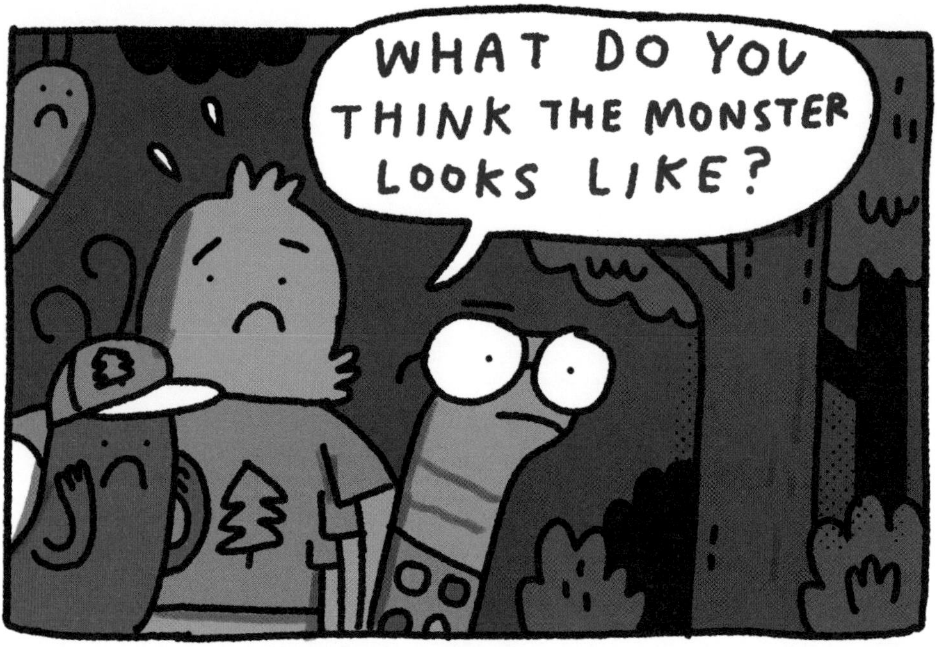
WHAT DO YOU THINK THE MONSTER LOOKS LIKE?

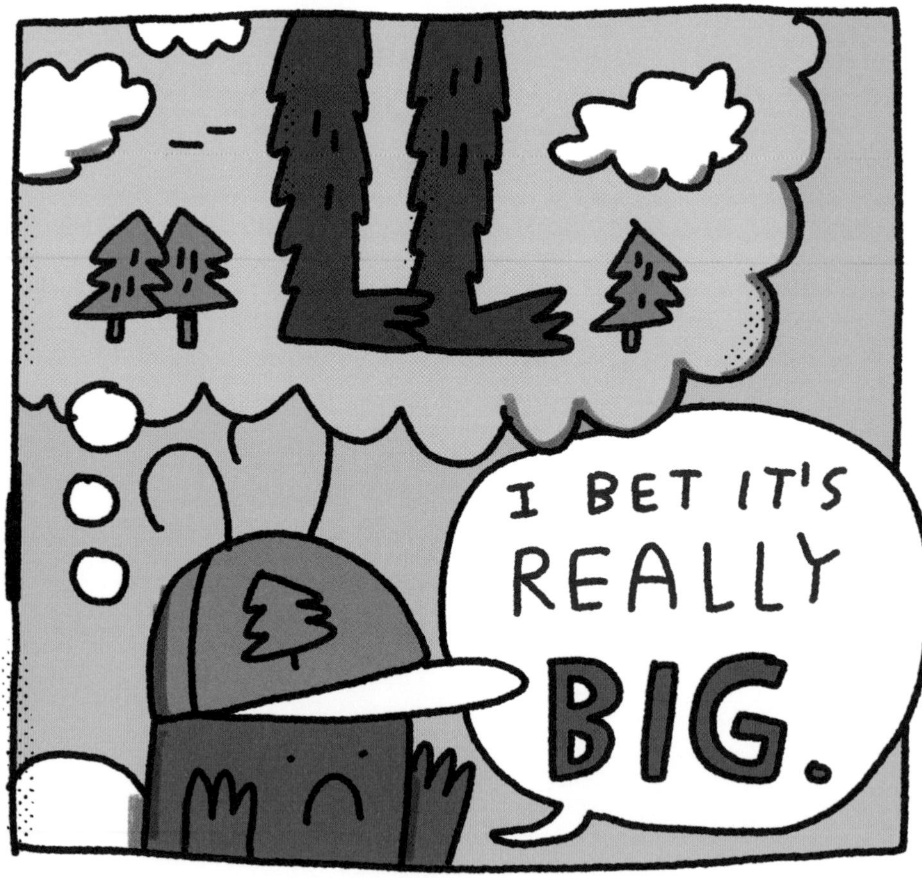
I BET IT'S REALLY BIG.

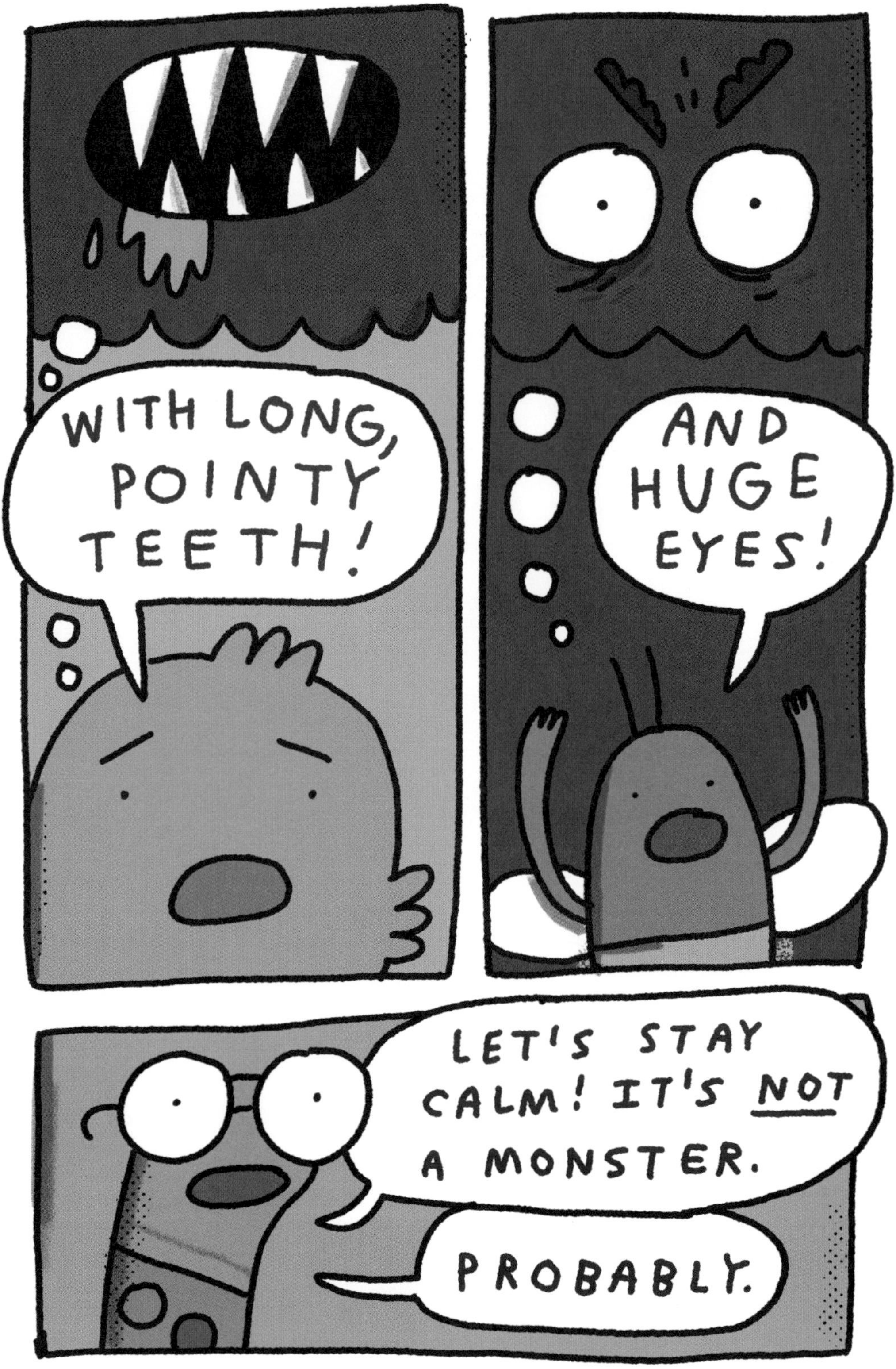
WITH LONG, POINTY TEETH!
AND HUGE EYES!
LET'S STAY CALM! IT'S NOT A MONSTER.
PROBABLY.

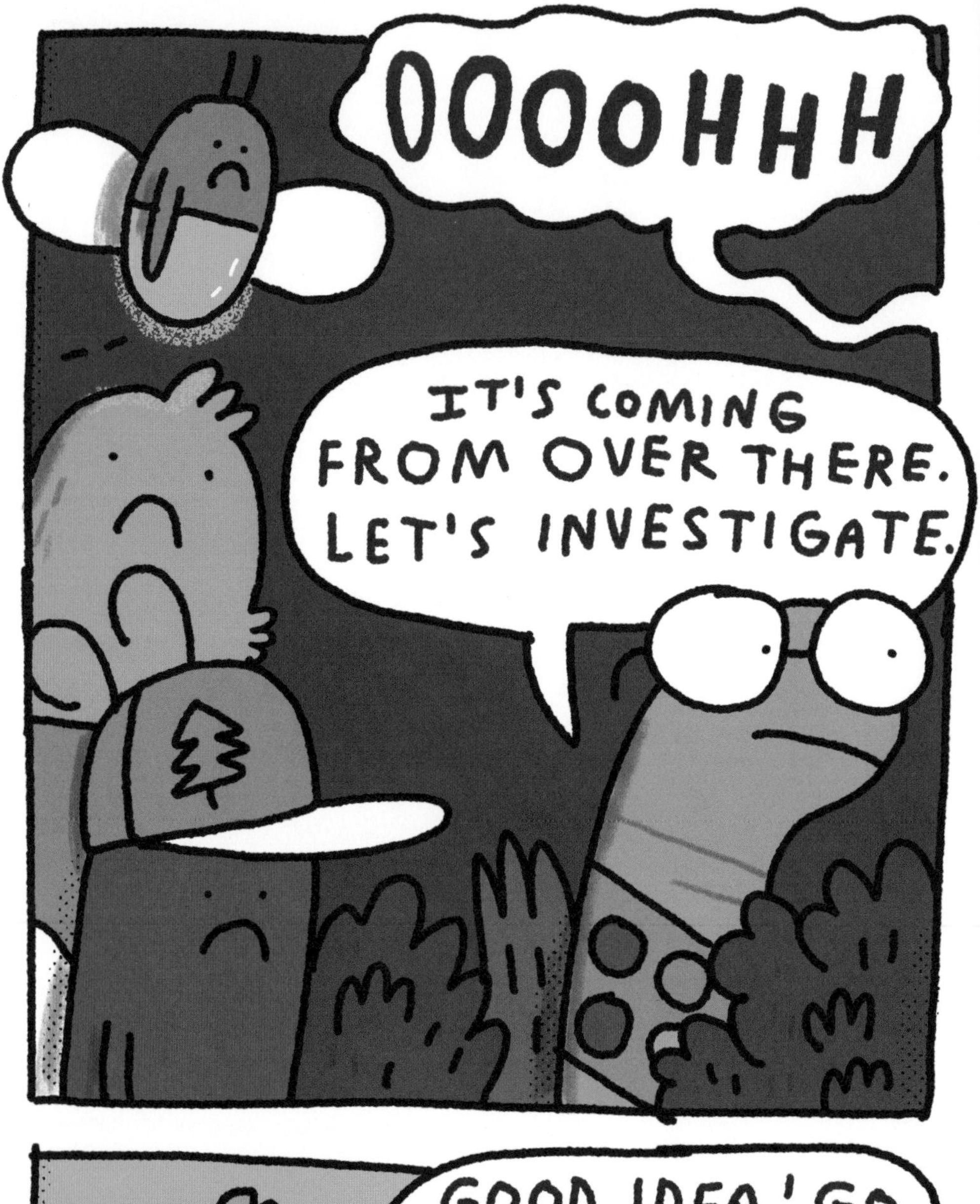
OOOOHHH
IT'S COMING FROM OVER THERE. LET'S INVESTIGATE.

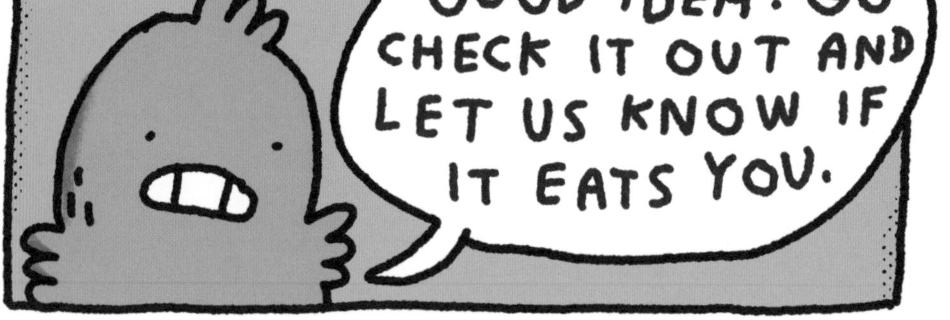
GOOD IDEA! GO CHECK IT OUT AND LET US KNOW IF IT EATS YOU.

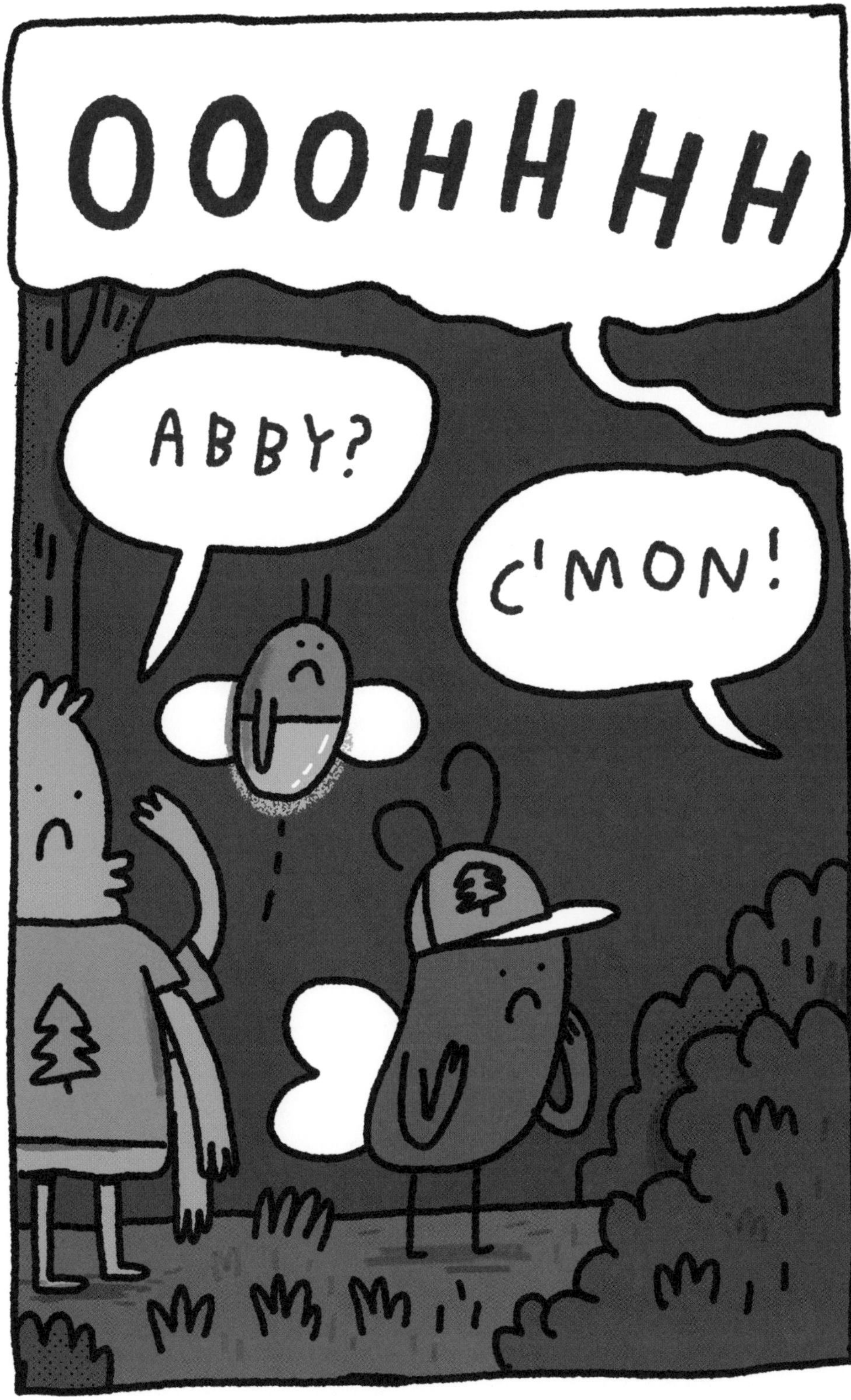
OOOHHHHH
ABBY?
C'MON!

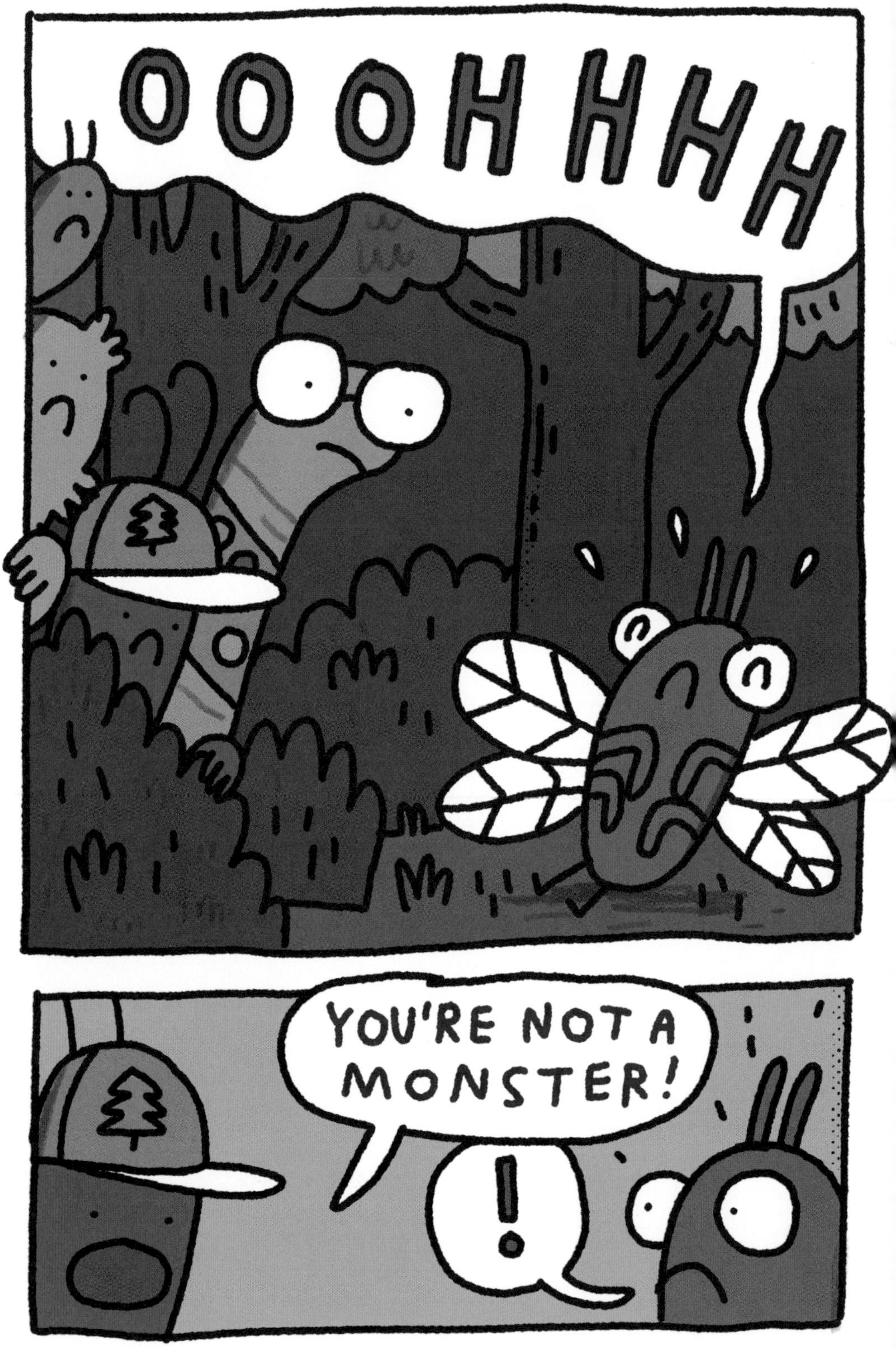
OOOHHHHH
YOU'RE NOT A MONSTER!
!

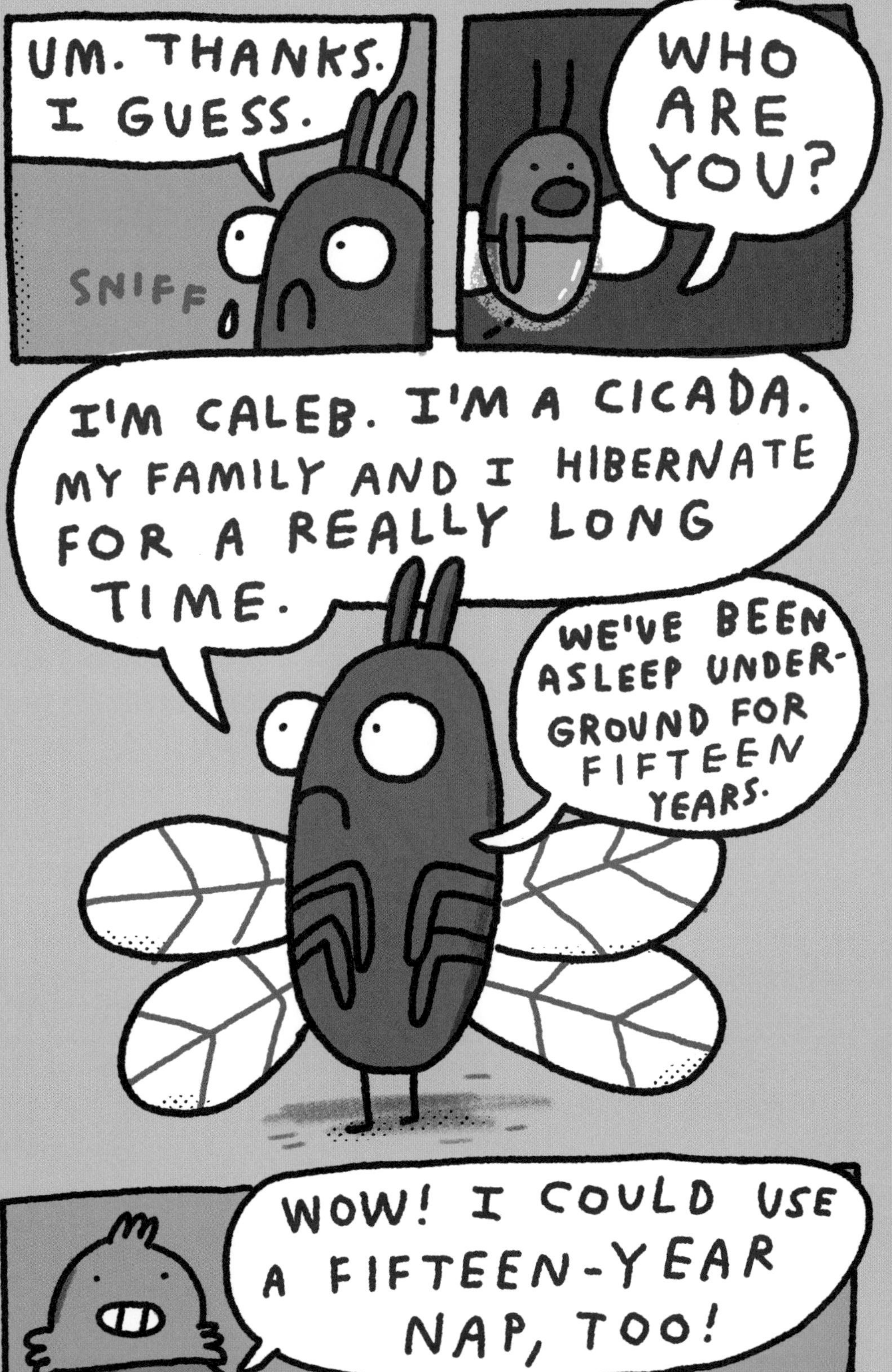
UM. THANKS. I GUESS.
SNIFF
WHO ARE YOU?
I'M CALEB. I'M A CICADA. MY FAMILY AND I HIBERNATE FOR A REALLY LONG TIME.
WE'VE BEEN ASLEEP UNDER-GROUND FOR FIFTEEN YEARS.
WOW! I COULD USE A FIFTEEN-YEAR NAP, TOO!

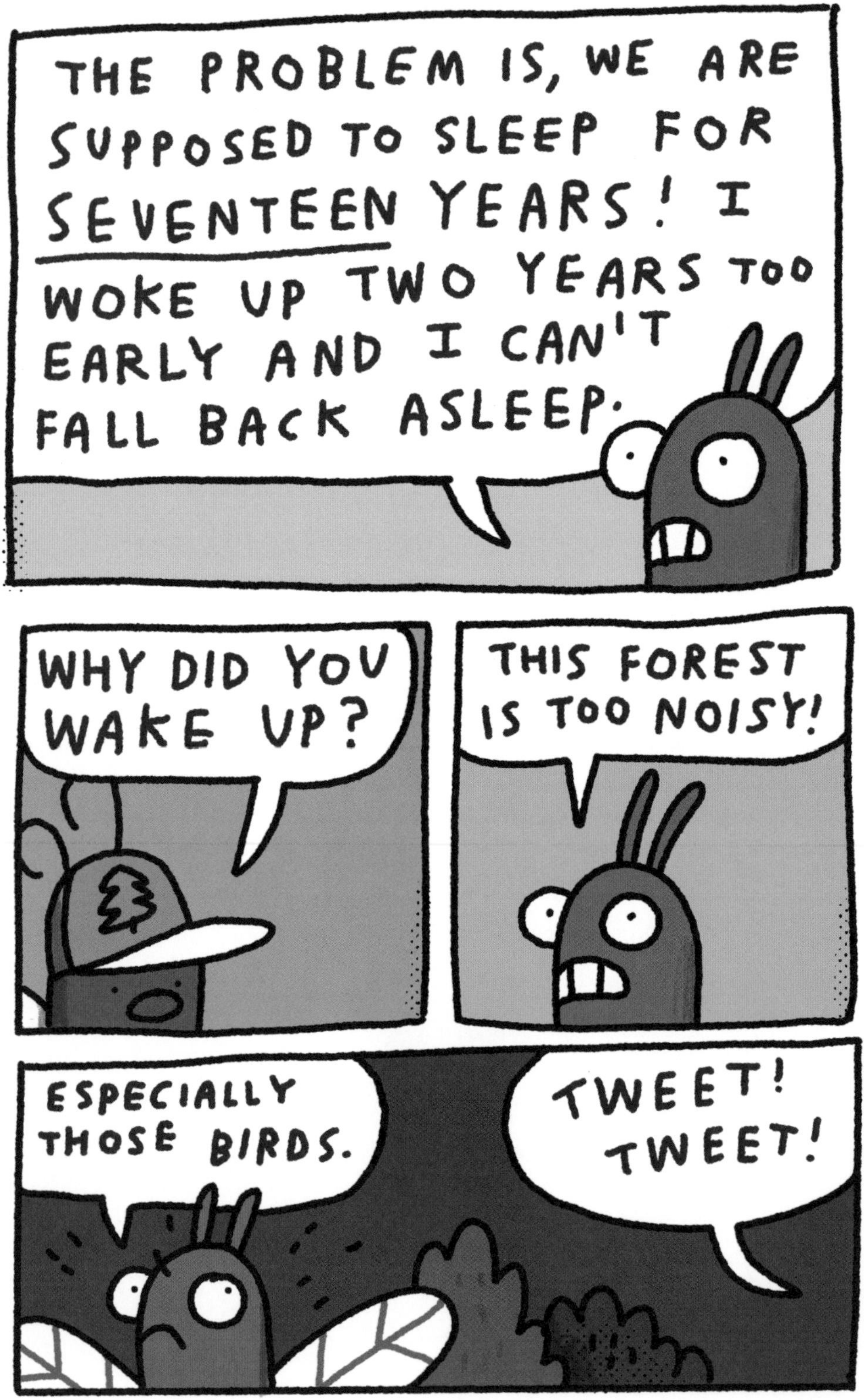
THE PROBLEM IS, WE ARE SUPPOSED TO SLEEP FOR SEVENTEEN YEARS! I WOKE UP TWO YEARS TOO EARLY AND I CAN'T FALL BACK ASLEEP.
WHY DID YOU WAKE UP?
THIS FOREST IS TOO NOISY!
ESPECIALLY THOSE BIRDS.
TWEET! TWEET!

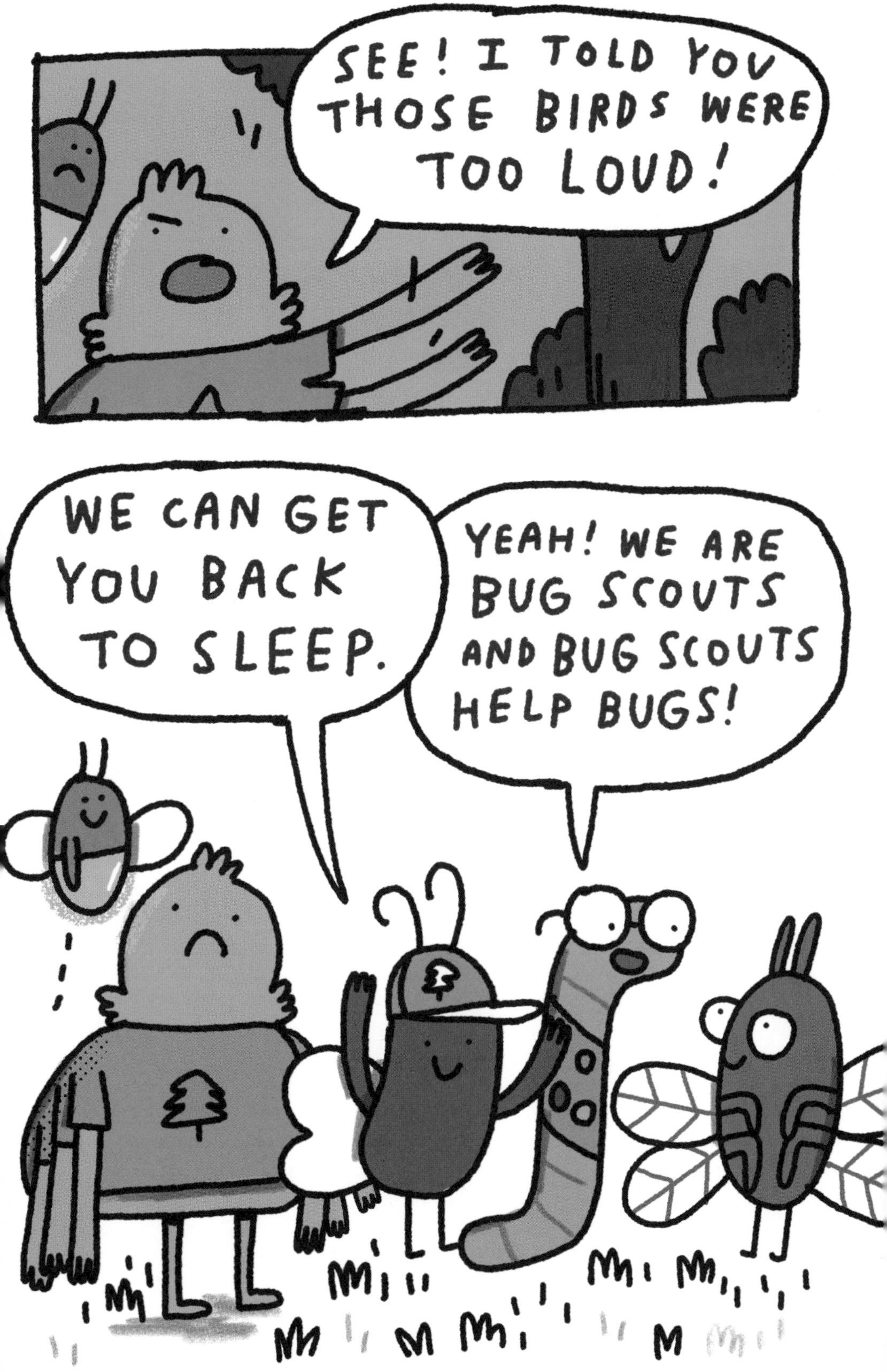
SEE! I TOLD YOU THOSE BIRDS WERE TOO LOUD!
WE CAN GET YOU BACK TO SLEEP.
YEAH! WE ARE BUG SCOUTS AND BUG SCOUTS HELP BUGS!

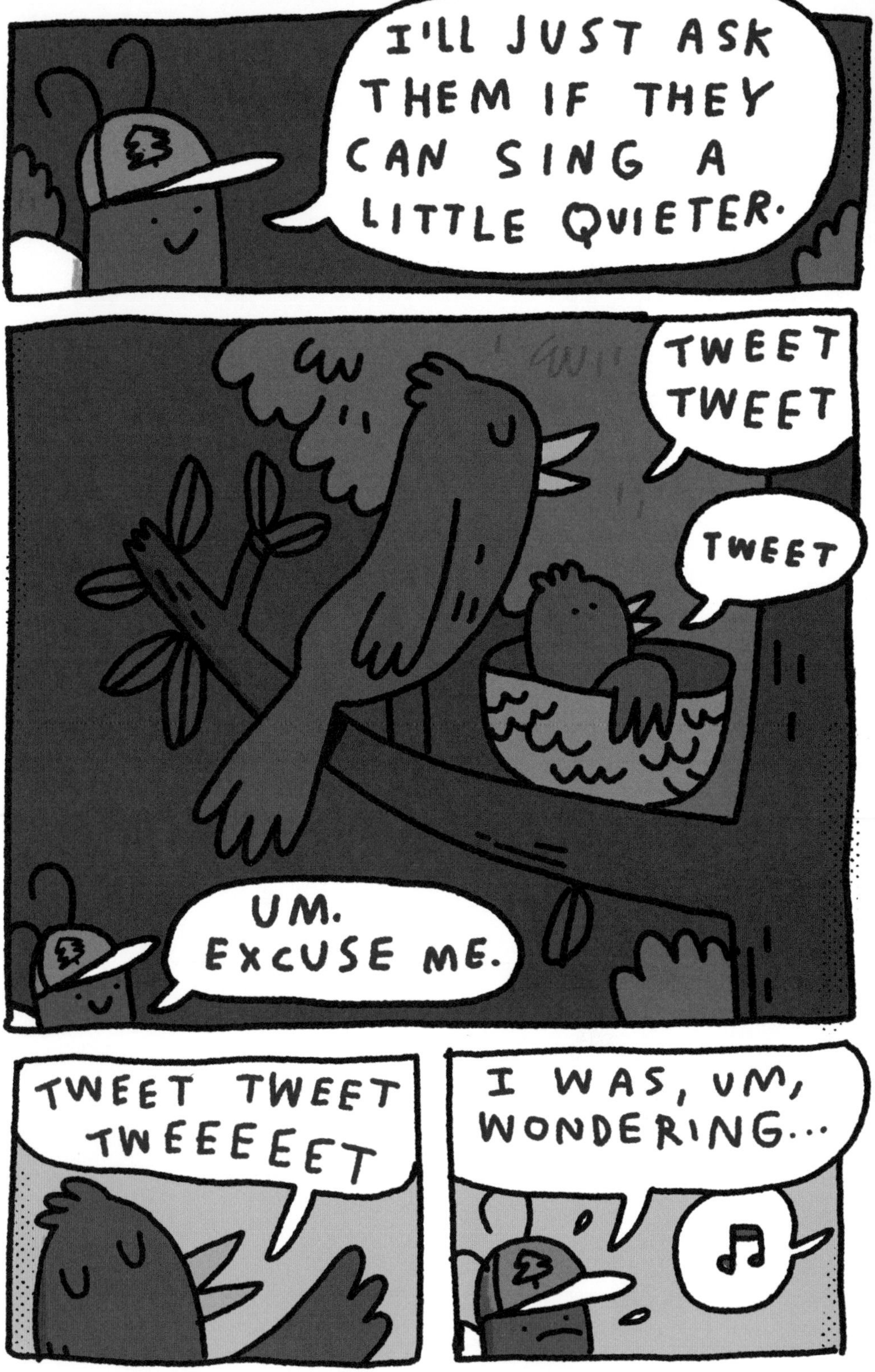
I'LL JUST ASK THEM IF THEY CAN SING A LITTLE QUIETER.
TWEET TWEET
TWEET
UM. EXCUSE ME.
TWEET TWEET TWEEEEEET
I WAS, UM, WONDERING...

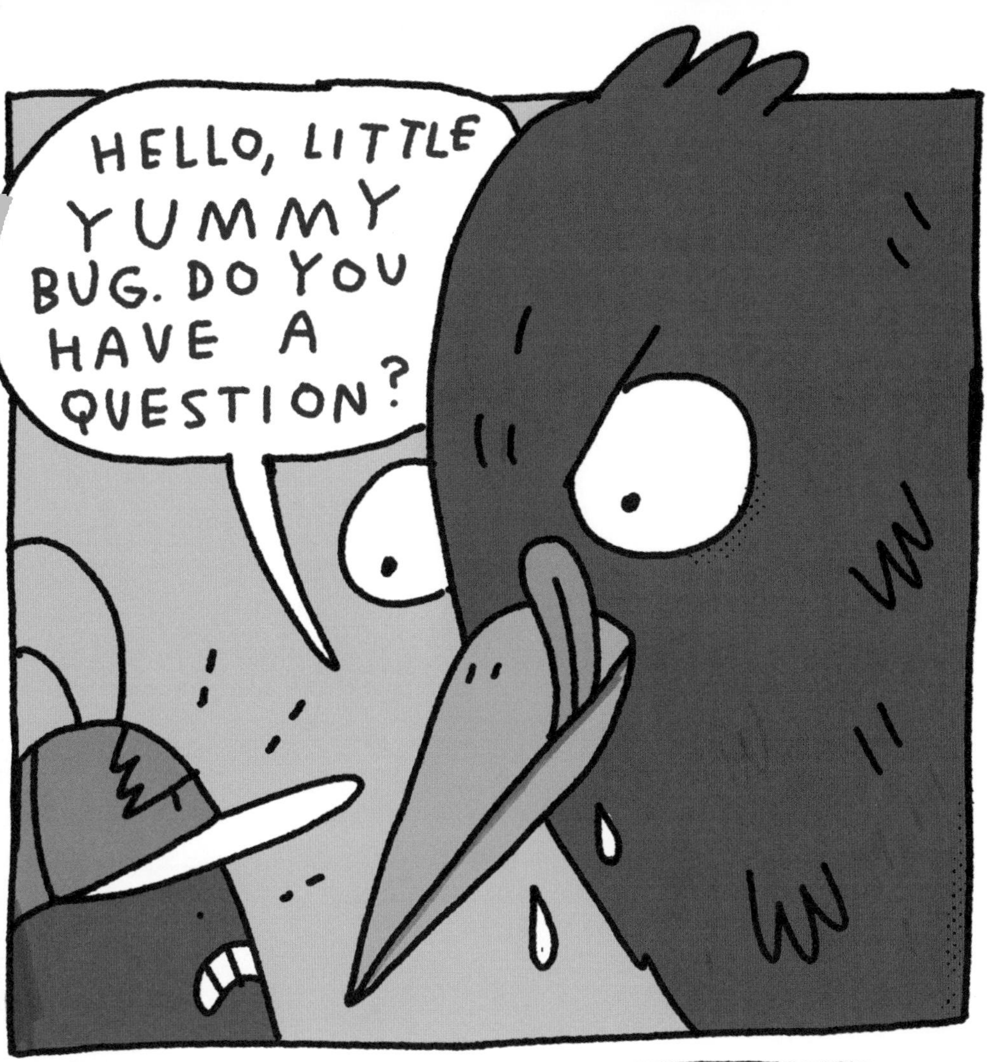
HELLO, LITTLE YUMMY BUG. DO YOU HAVE A QUESTION?

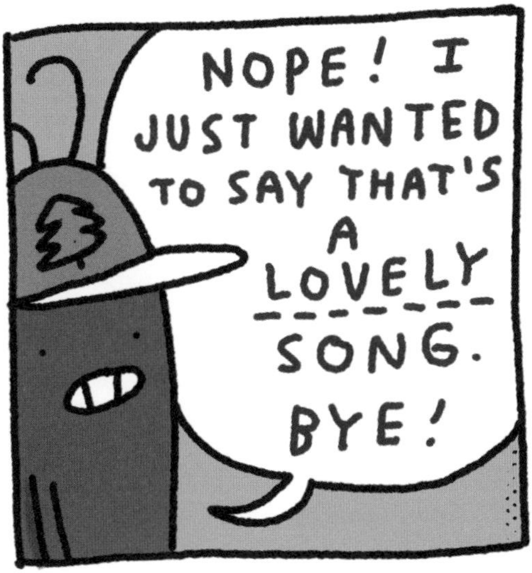
NOPE! I JUST WANTED TO SAY THAT'S A LOVELY SONG. BYE!

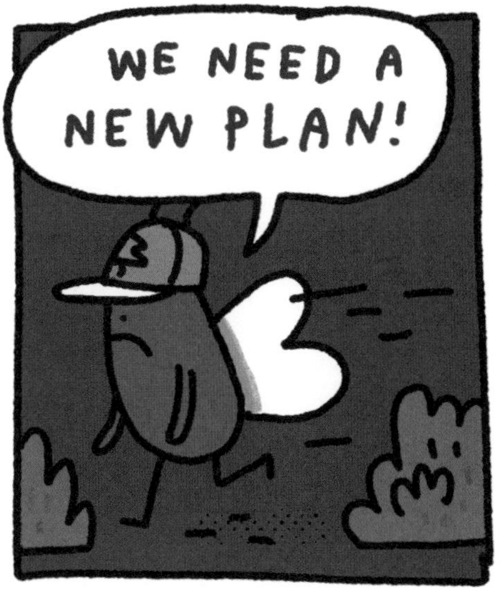
WE NEED A NEW PLAN!

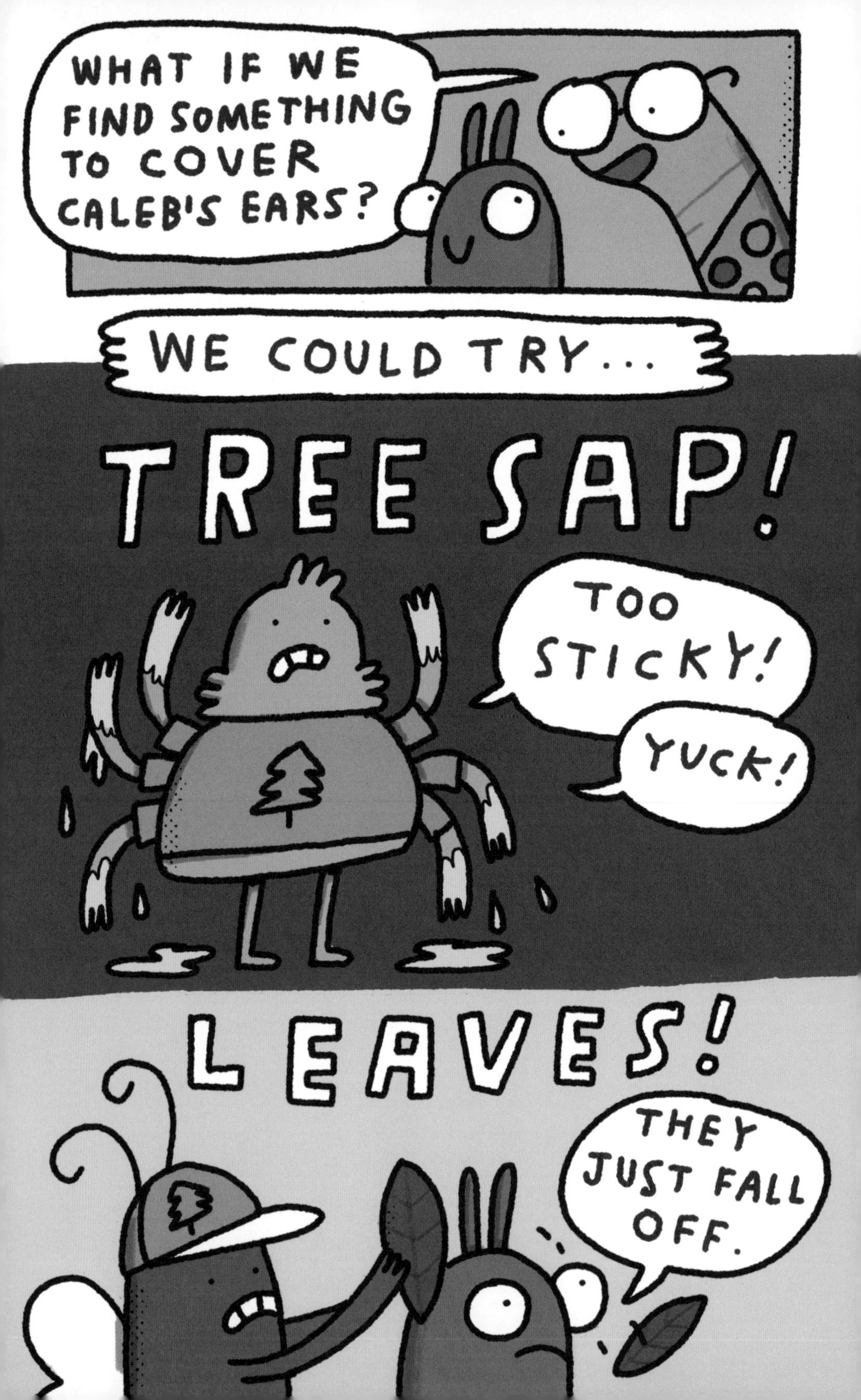
WHAT IF WE FIND SOMETHING TO COVER CALEB'S EARS?
WE COULD TRY...
TREE SAP!
TOO STICKY!
YUCK!
LEAVES!
THEY JUST FALL OFF.

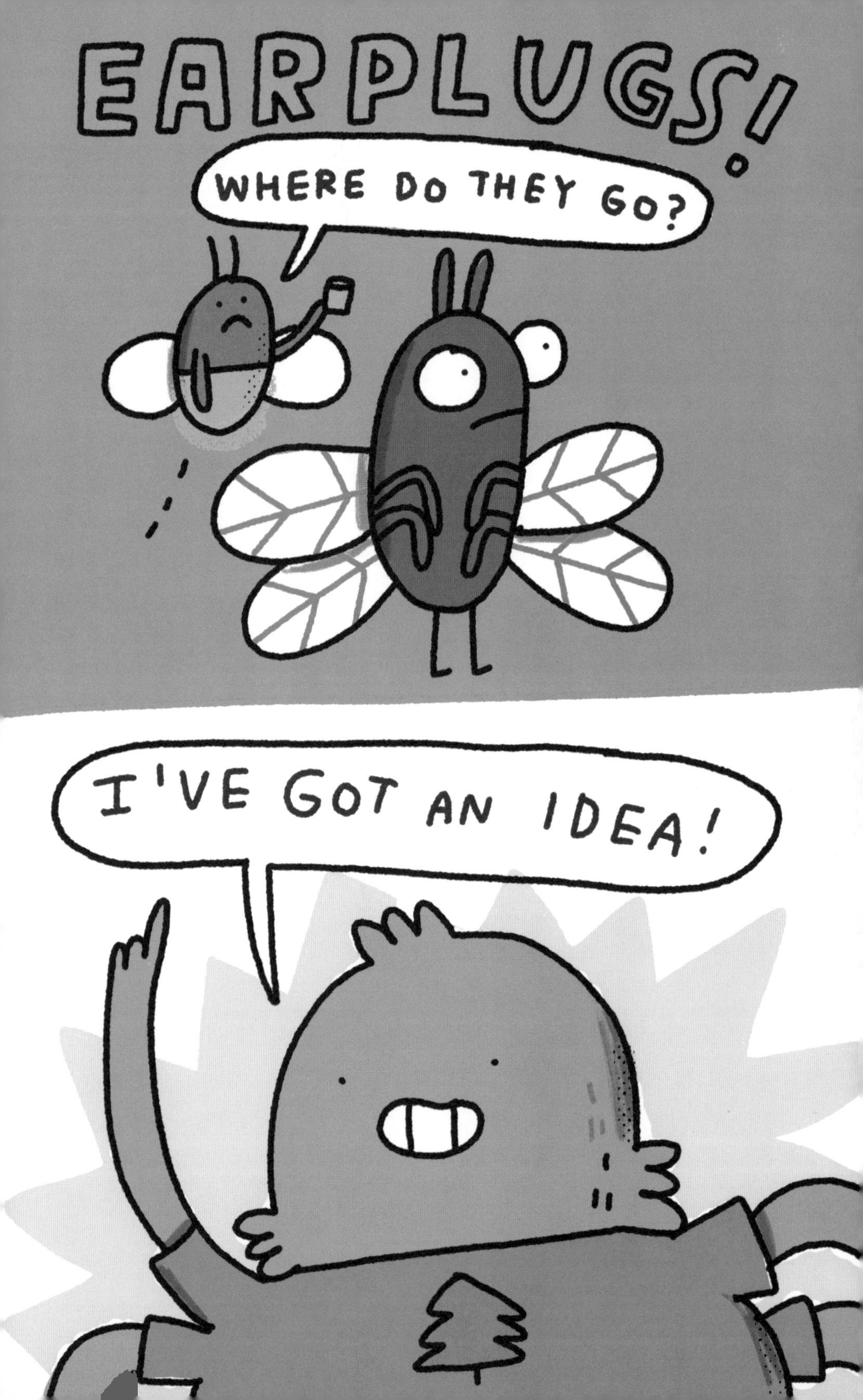
EARPLUGS!
WHERE DO THEY GO?
I'VE GOT AN IDEA!

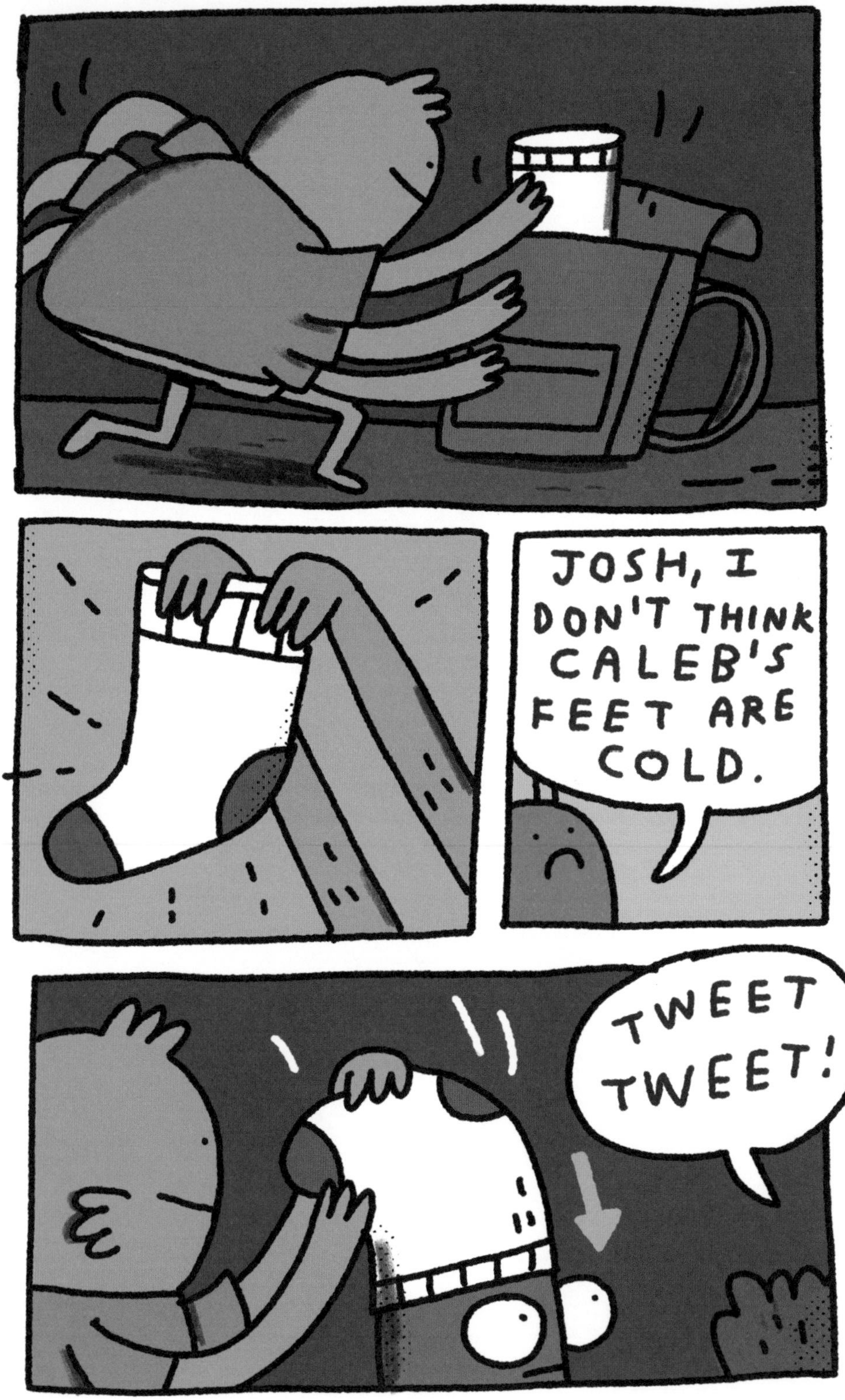
JOSH, I DON'T THINK CALEB'S FEET ARE COLD.
TWEET TWEET!

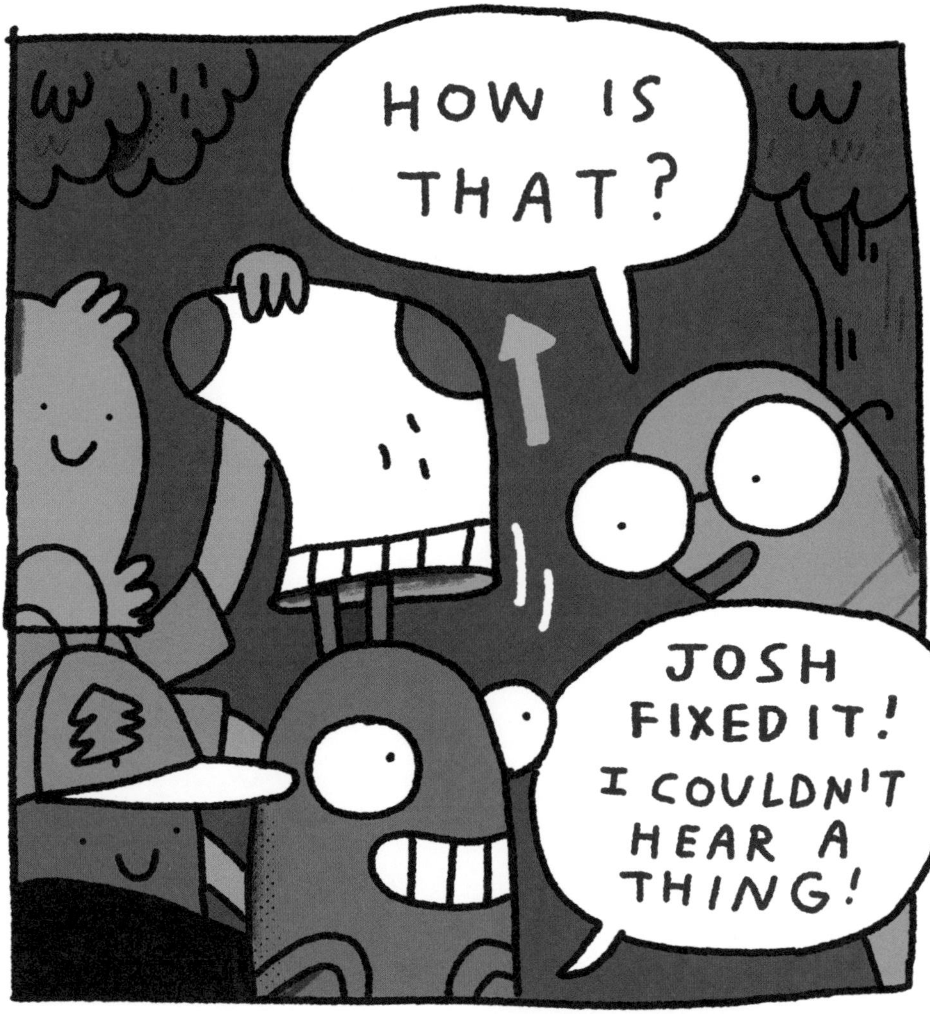
HOW IS THAT?
JOSH FIXED IT! I COULDN'T HEAR A THING!

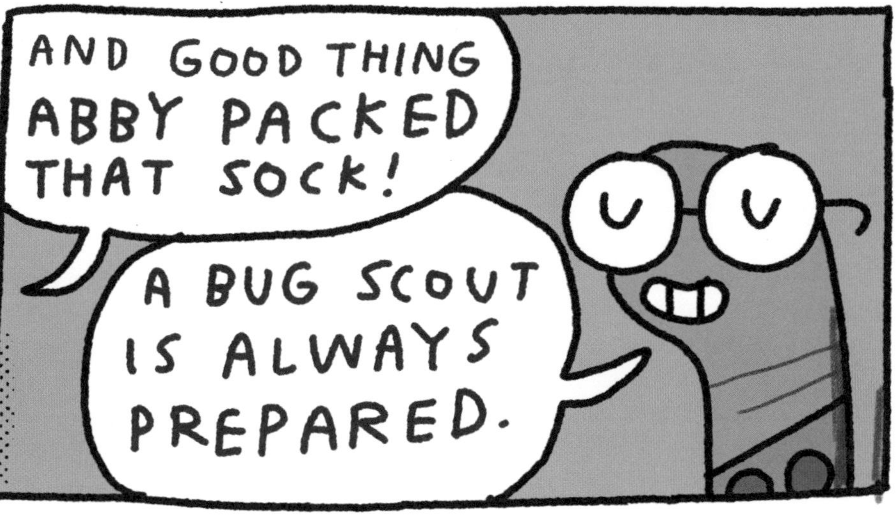
AND GOOD THING ABBY PACKED THAT SOCK!
A BUG SCOUT IS ALWAYS PREPARED.

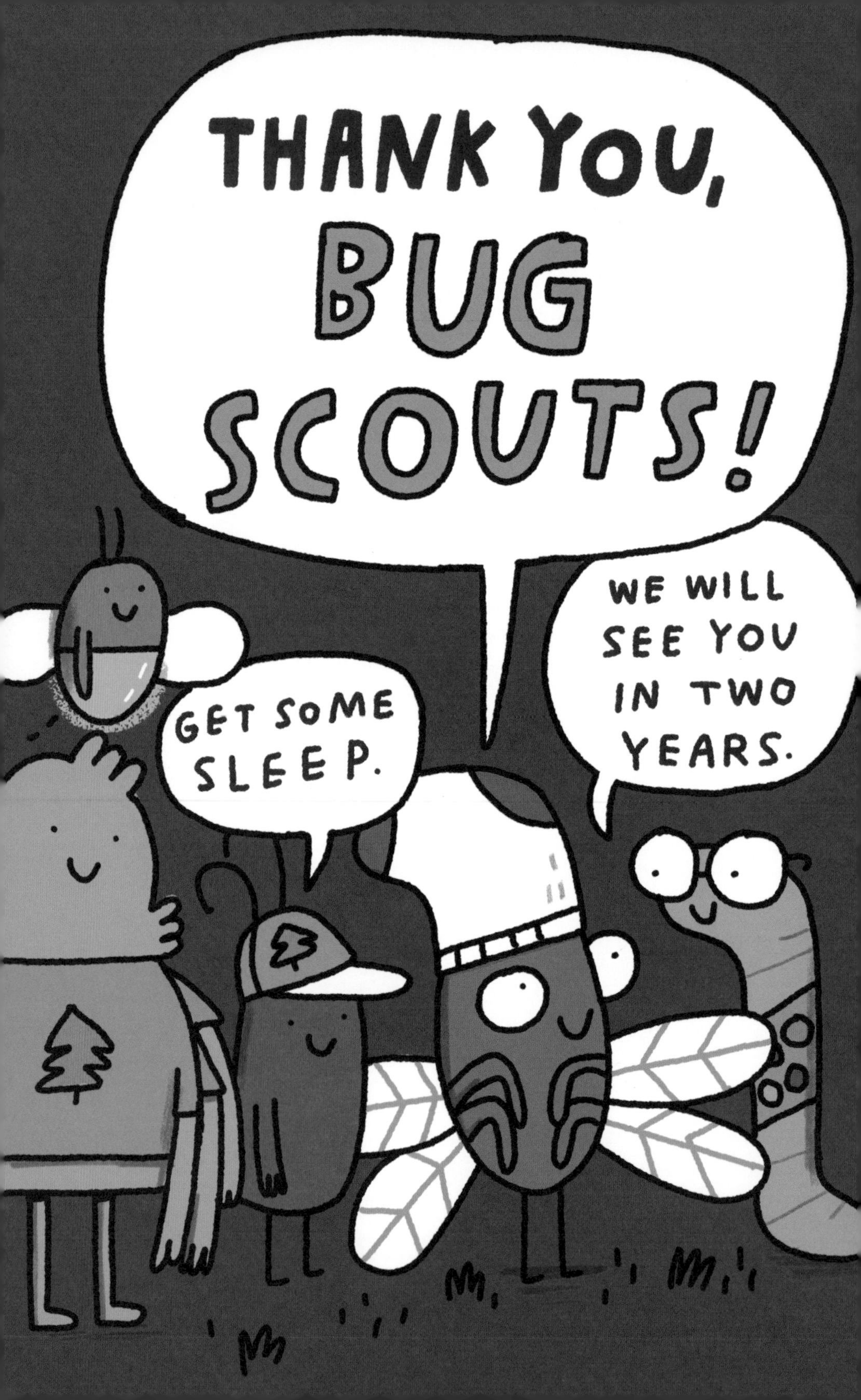
THANK YOU, BUG SCOUTS!
GET SOME SLEEP.
WE WILL SEE YOU IN TWO YEARS.

CHAPTER

5

MAKING

S'NORES

ZZZ

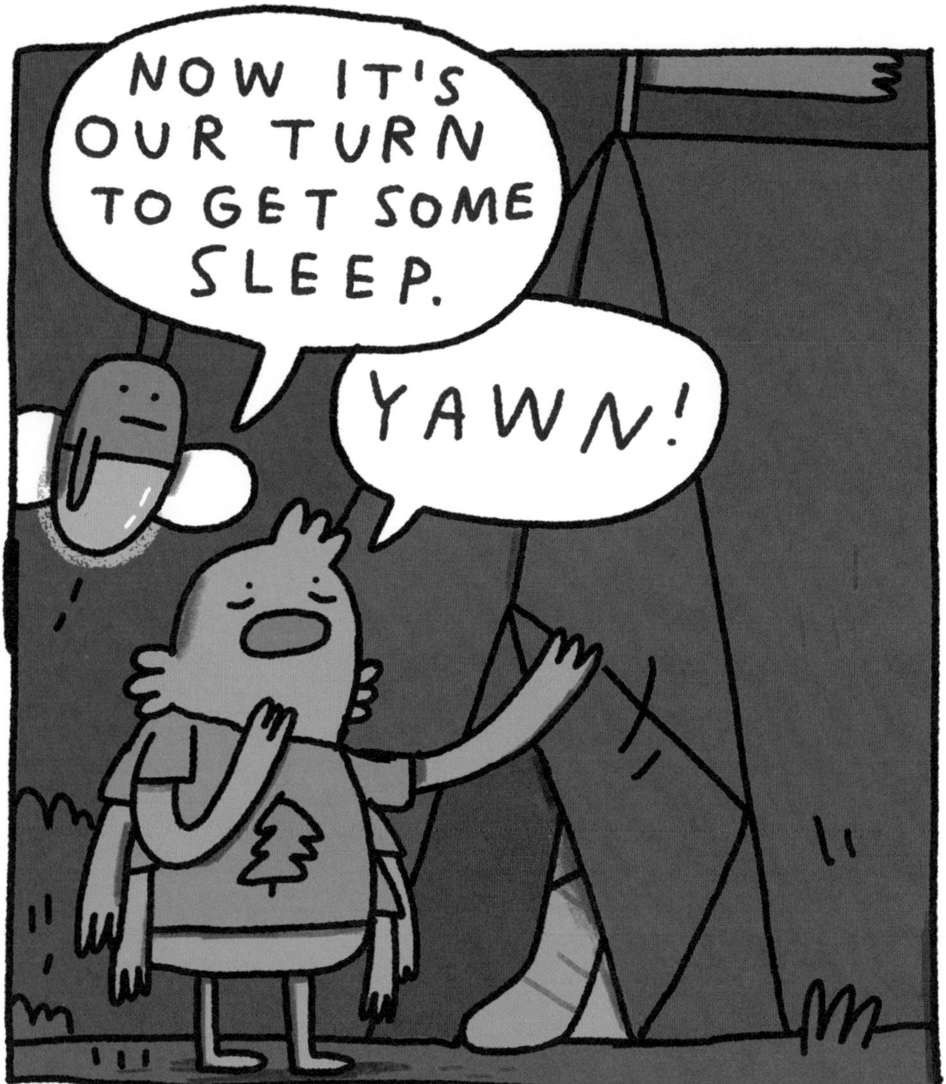
NOW IT'S OUR TURN TO GET SOME SLEEP.
YAWN!

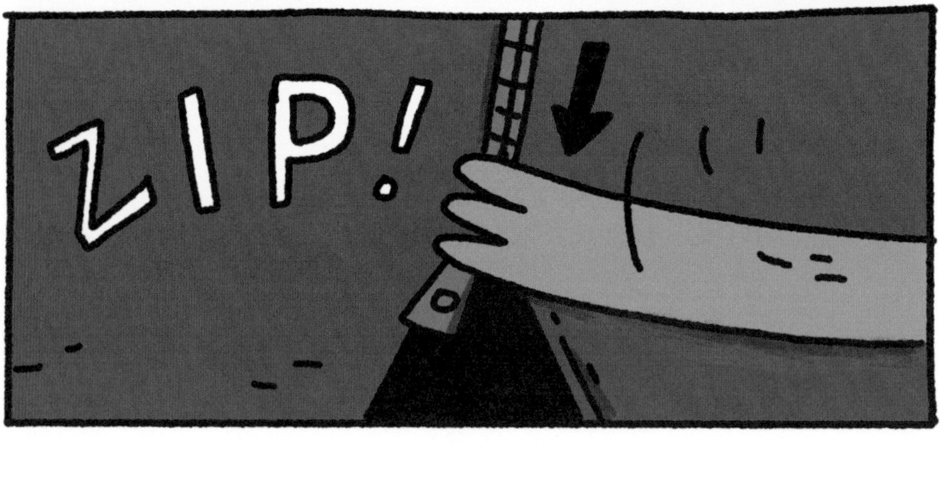
ZIP!

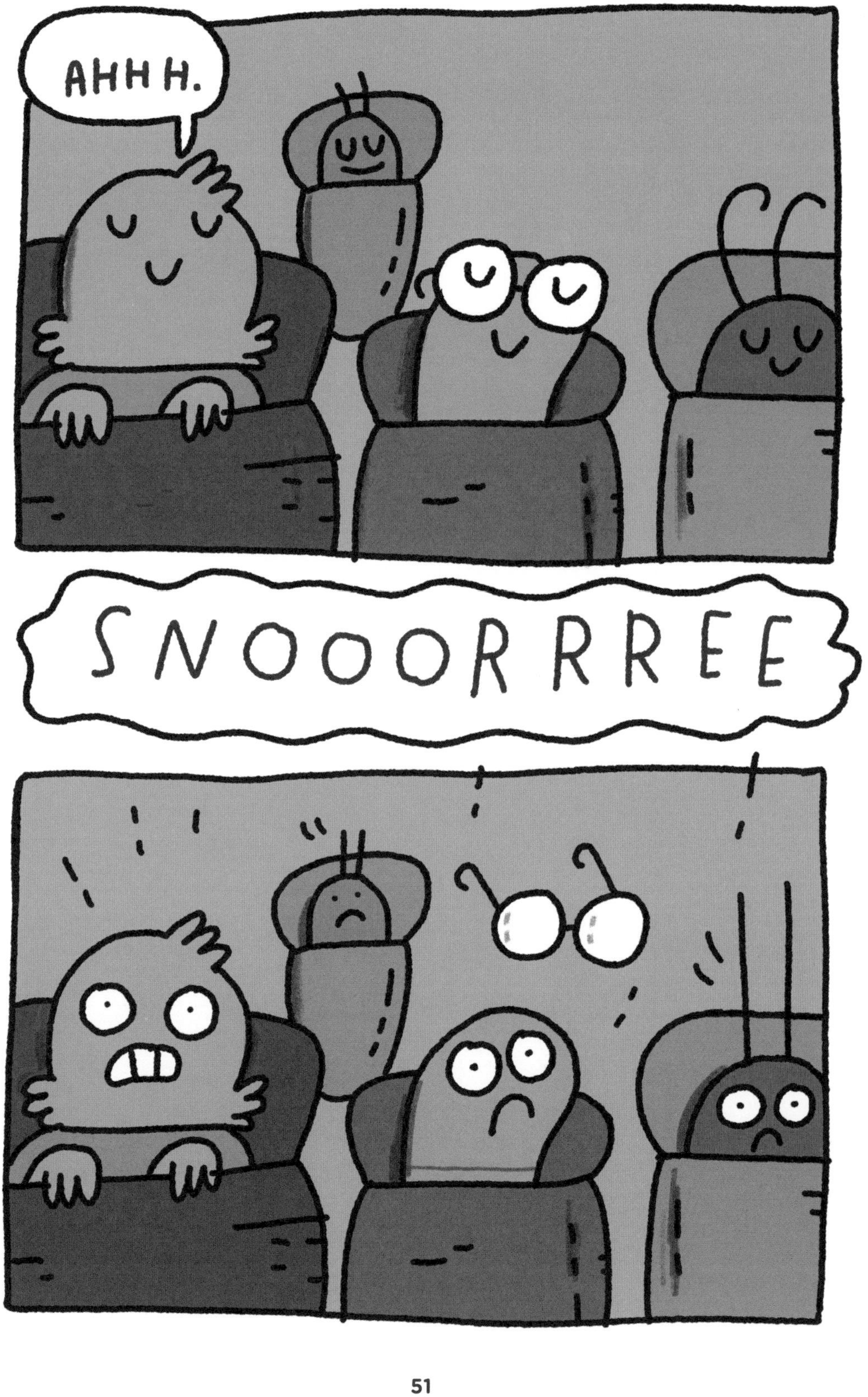
AHHH.
SNOOORRREE

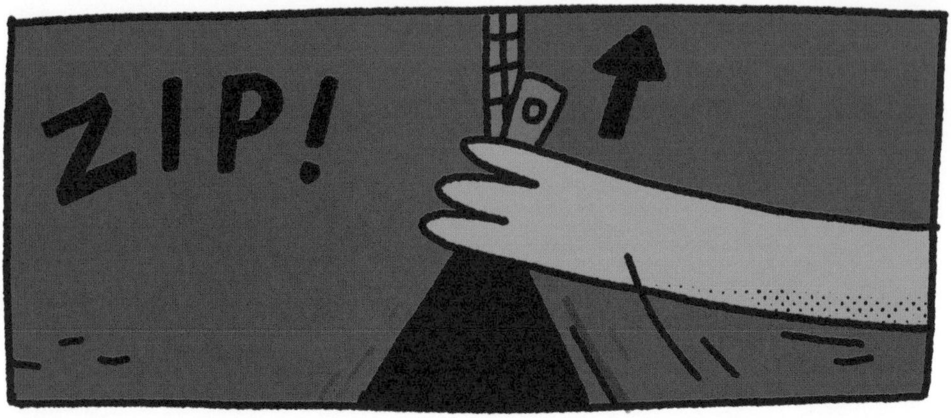
ZIP!

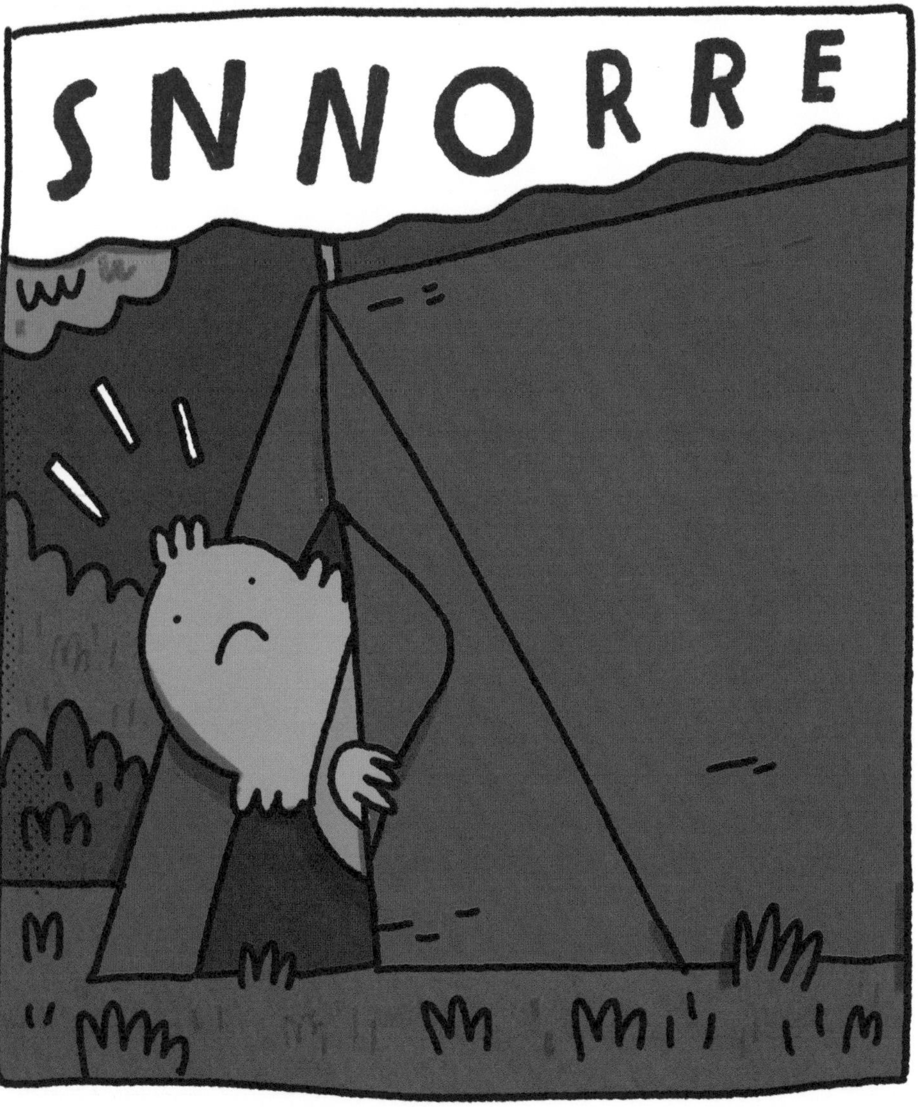
SNNORRE

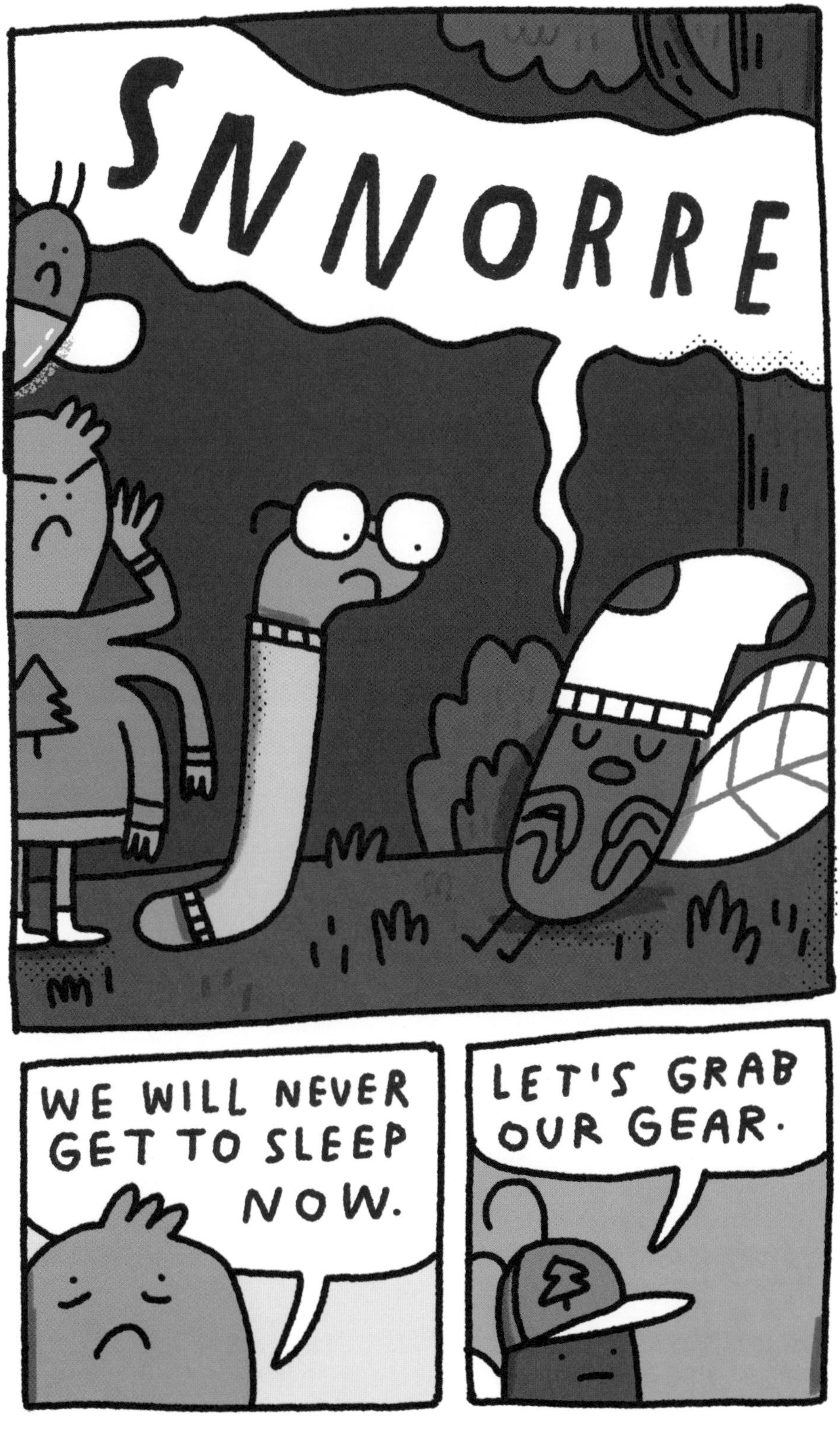
SNNORRE
WE WILL NEVER GET TO SLEEP NOW.
LET'S GRAB OUR GEAR.

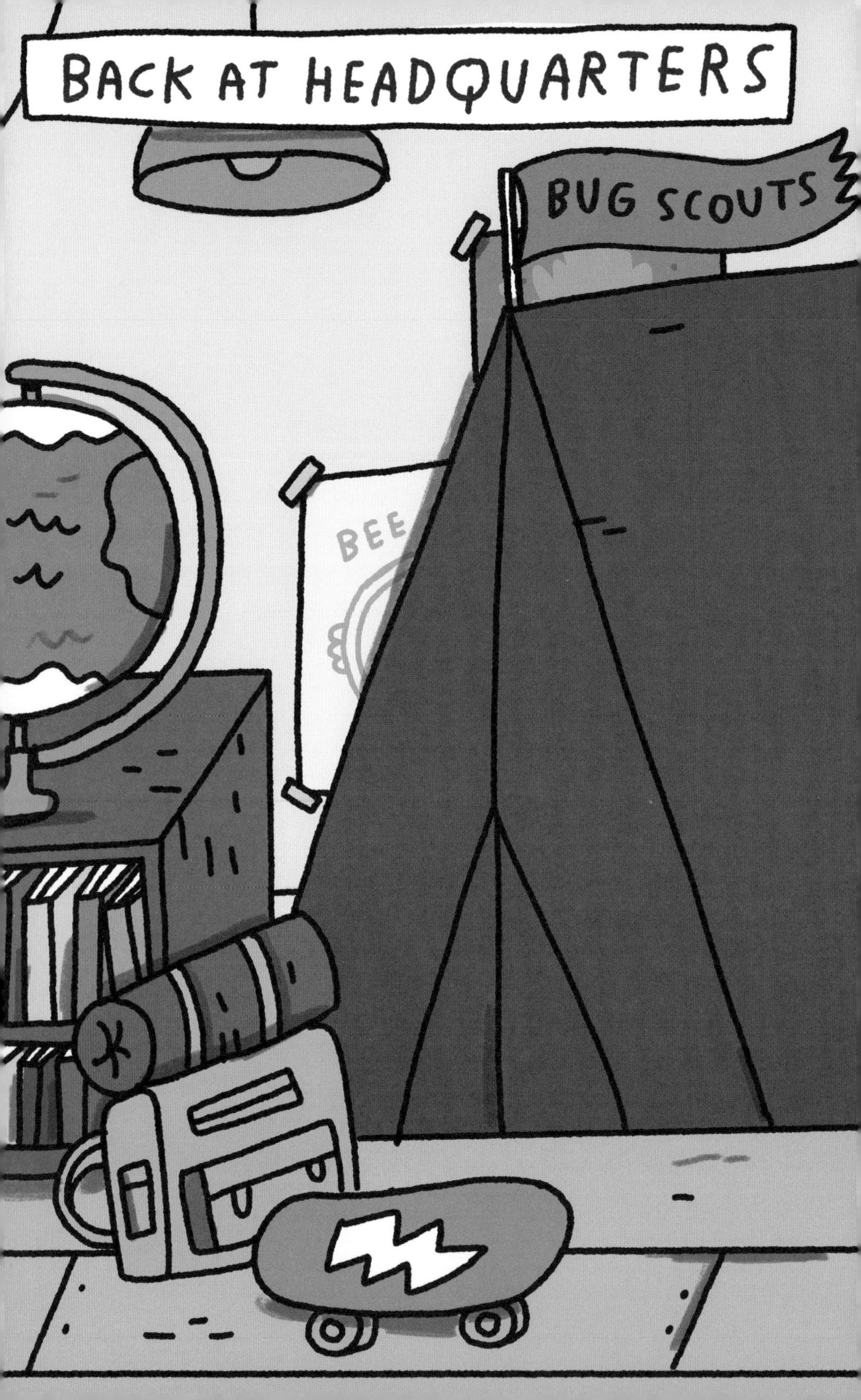
BACK AT HEADQUARTERS
BUG SCOUTS
BEE

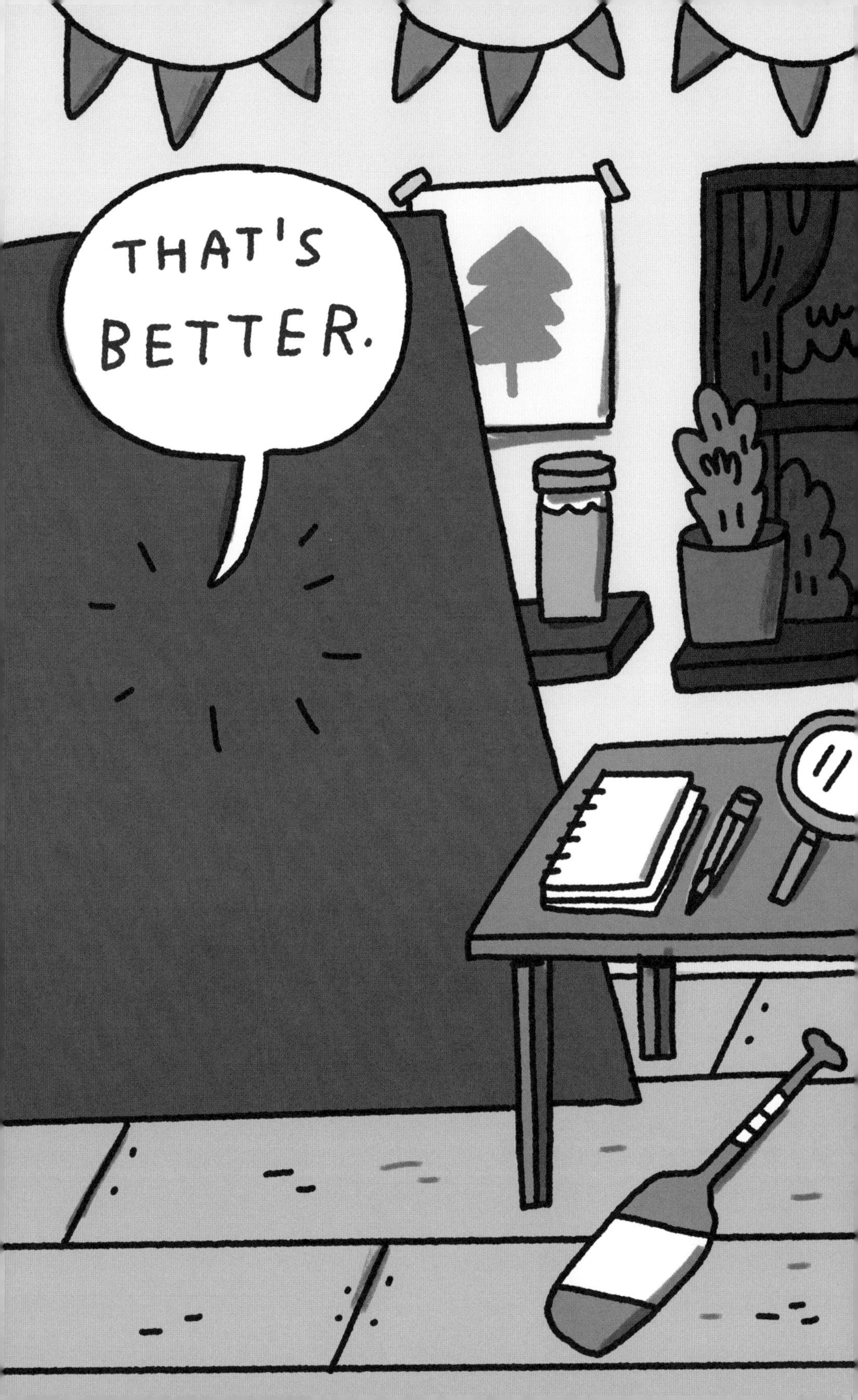
THAT'S BETTER.

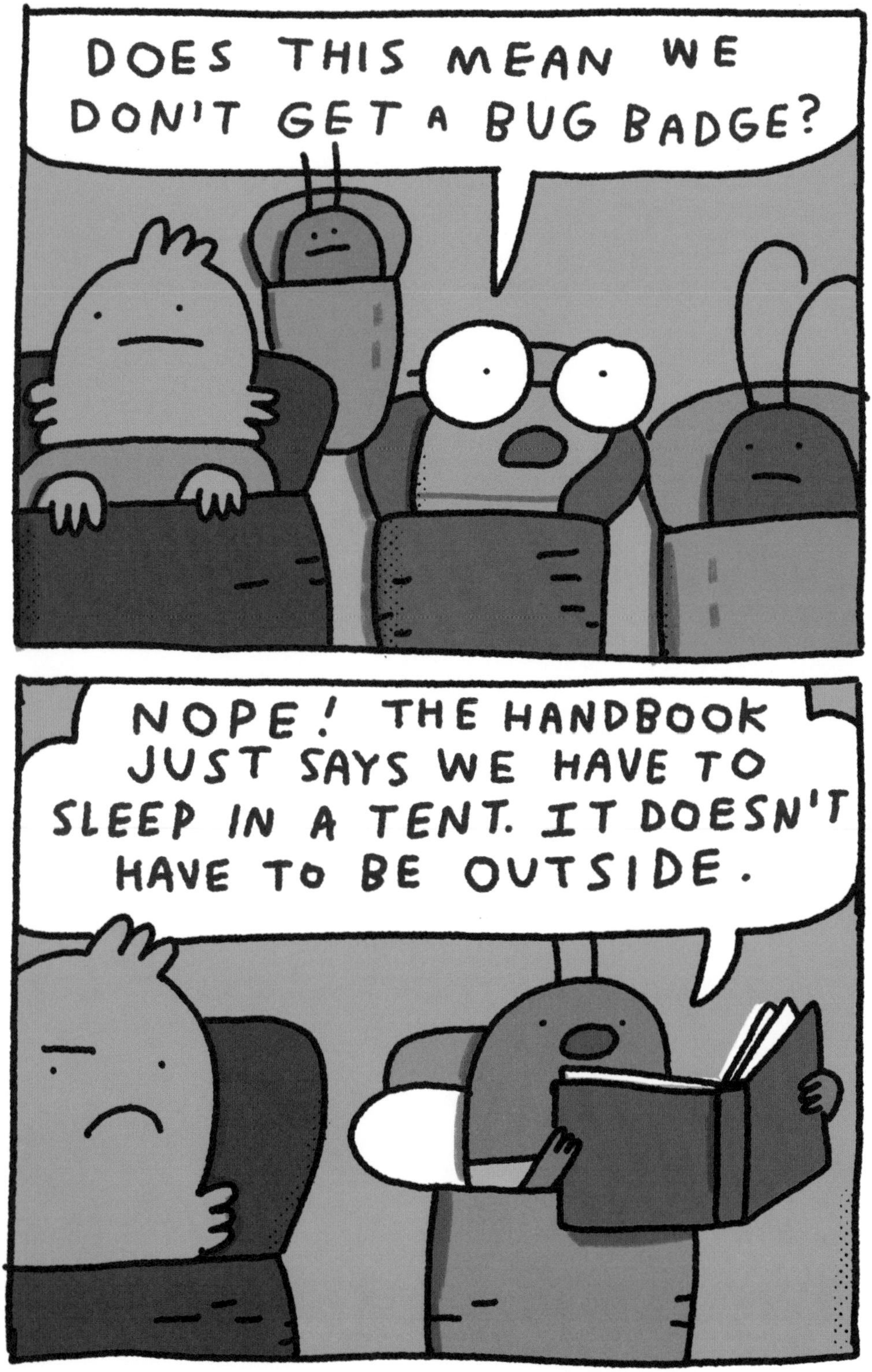
DOES THIS MEAN WE DON'T GET A BUG BADGE?
NOPE! THE HANDBOOK JUST SAYS WE HAVE TO SLEEP IN A TENT. IT DOESN'T HAVE TO BE OUTSIDE.

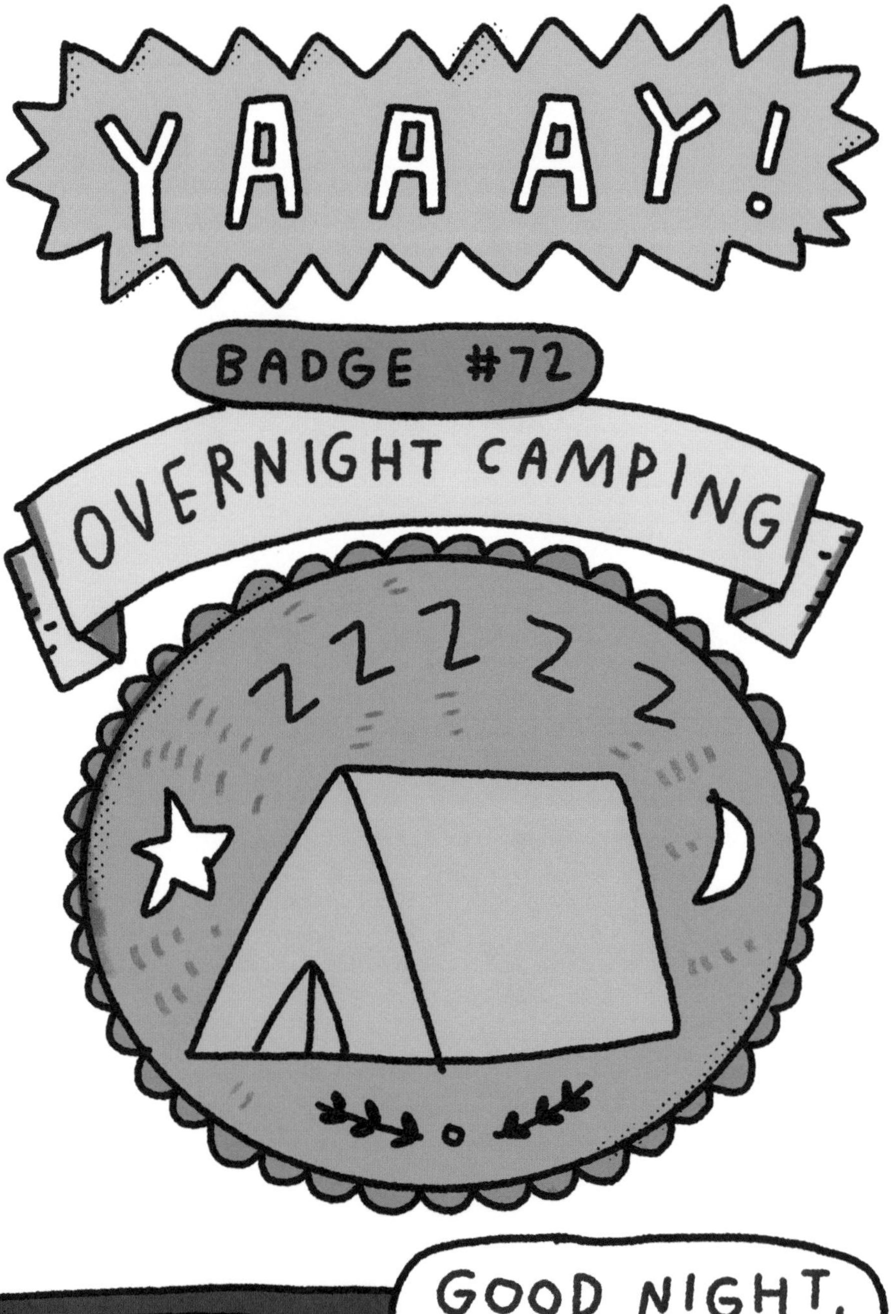
YAAAY!
BADGE #72
OVERNIGHT CAMPING
ZZZZZZ

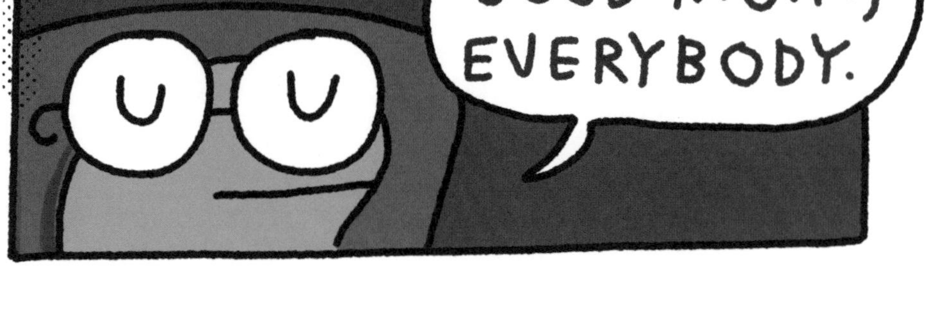
GOOD NIGHT, EVERYBODY.

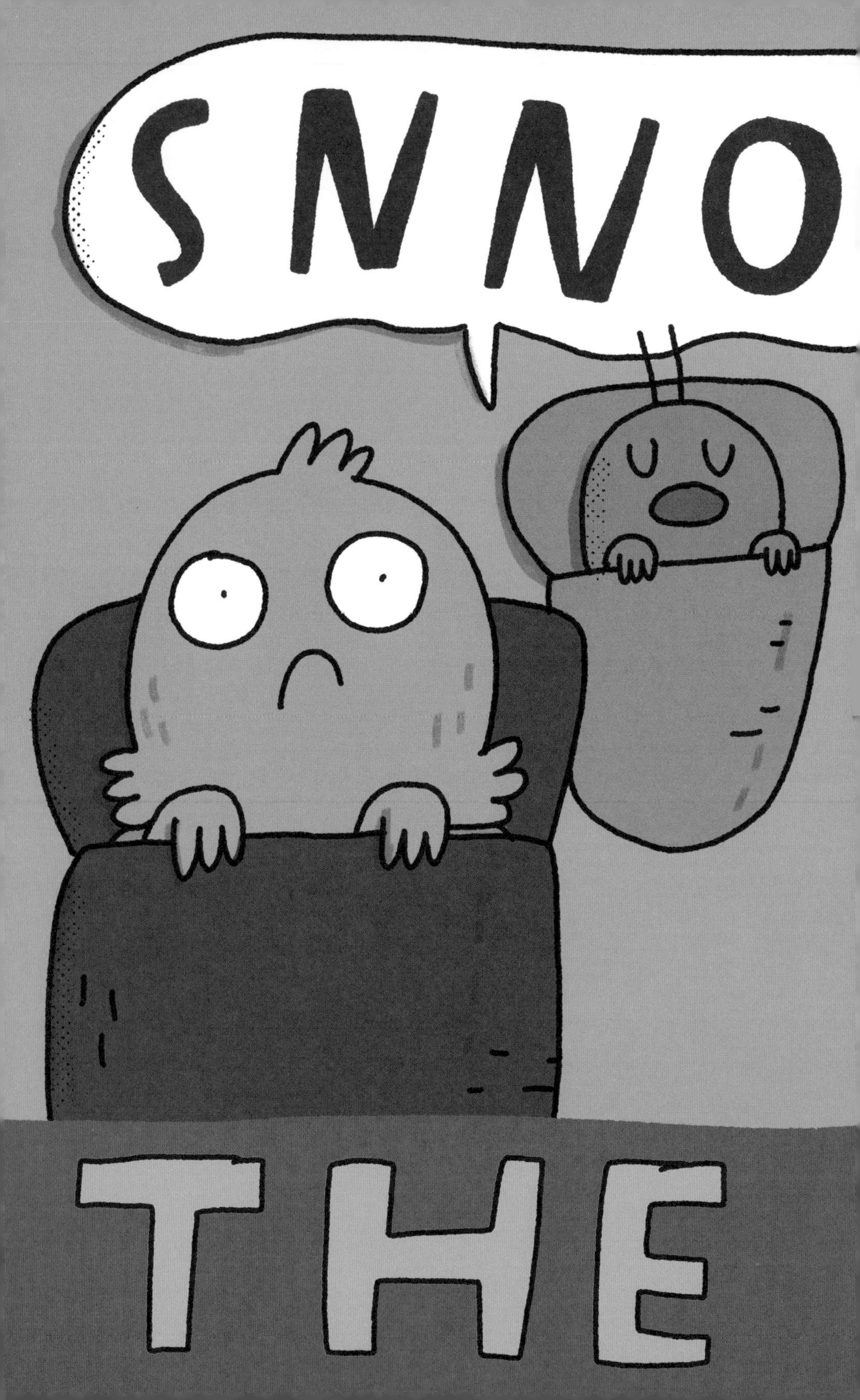
SNNO
THE

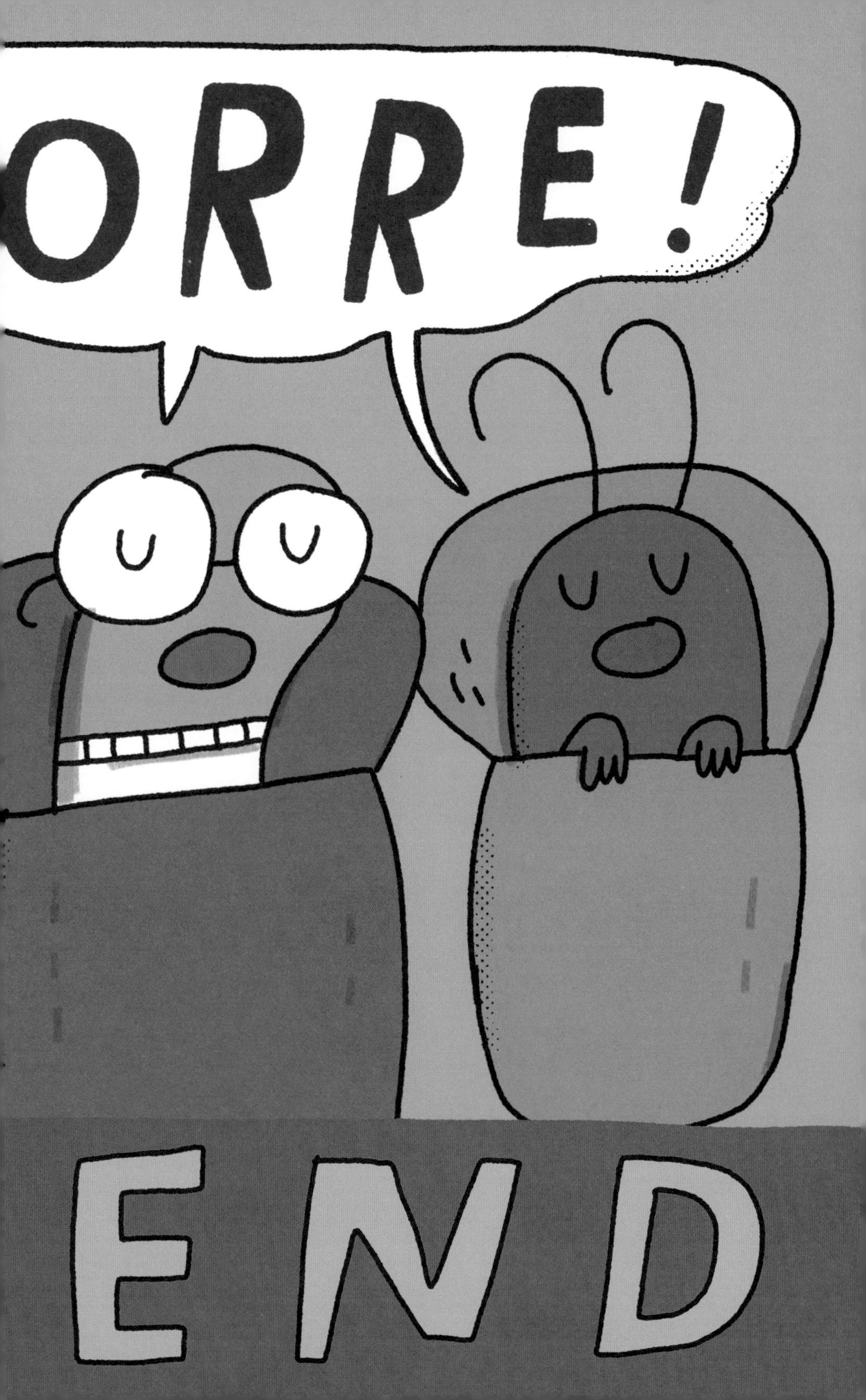

ORRE!
END

MIKE LOWERY

is the illustrator of many books for kids, including the *New York Times*–bestselling Mac B., Kid Spy books. He is also the creator of the Everything Awesome books. He lives in Atlanta with his amazing wife and super-genius kids. He collects weird facts and draws them every day in his sketchbook. See them on Instagram at: @mikelowerystudio.